CHRISTMAS
of the
CHERRY
SNOW

CHRISTMAS of the CHERRY SNOW

RICHARD M. SIDDOWAY

EAGLE
GATE

SALT LAKE CITY, UTAH

Library of Congress Cataloging-in-Publication Data

Siddoway, Richard M.
  Christmas of the cherry snow / Richard M. Siddoway.
      p.   cm.
  ISBN 1-57345-906-2 (Hardbound : alk. paper)
  1. Accident victims—Family relationships—Fiction.
2. Coma—Patients—Fiction.   3. Teenage boys—Fiction.
4. Family farms—Fiction.   5. Orchards—Fiction.   I. Title
PS3569.I29 C45 2001
813'.54—dc21

                                                    2001000811

Printed in the United States of America   72876-6782
10 9   8   7   6   5   4   3   2   1

*To my wife, Janice, who exhibits
faith in all she does.*

*To Richard Peterson, a wonderful editor and friend,
and the others at Eagle Gate who continually
exhibit faith in their authors.*

*And to the unknown fan in Topeka, Kansas,
who told me someone ought to write a book
about a Christmas Eve disaster.*

Thanks to you all.

PROLOGUE

MY GRANDDAUGHTER, Cassandra Jo, snuggled against me as we rocked slowly in the recliner.

"How's my favorite four-year-old?"

"'Most five, Grandpa," she said, burrowing under my arm. "Read me a story."

"What's the magic word, Cassie?" I asked.

"Puleez," she said, drawing it out like warm taffy.

I retrieved a stack of books from the lamp table. "Which story do you want? *Hop on Pop? Green Eggs and Ham?*"

Cassie shook her head vigorously, sending her pigtails flying. I ducked to one side to avoid being slapped in the face. "The Christmas one, Grandpa," she said, sorting through the pile of books until she found *Twelve Tales of Christmas*.

"Why Christmas, Cassie Jo? Christmas was over a month ago."

She pointed her little sausage-like finger at the patio window. "'Cause it's snowing, Grandpa."

The flakes were so large they looked like cotton balls drifting from the pewter skies. We rocked slowly in silence, watching the flakes quickly coat the deck behind our house. A great feeling of peace came over me as we sat comfortably together in our secure cocoon.

"It's pretty, Grandpa."

I nodded my head. "Yes it is, Cassie. Yes it is." I reached down and picked up the afghan that lay folded beside the chair. "Cold?"

Cassie nodded her head, and I spread the afghan over my legs and tucked it around my granddaughter. She sighed contentedly and snuggled against me. After a few minutes of silent rocking, the book dropped from her fingers, and I heard her breathing become more and more regular.

As daylight drifted into dusk and the snow continued to fall slowly and silently, we sat and rocked, and I thought of another Christmas and another snow from nearly fifty years before.

1

Robert, I NEED YOUR finger," my mother said. Dutifully, I put my index finger on the shiny red ribbon she had wrapped around the Christmas gift, slipping it out as she pulled the knot tight. "Just one more to go." She completed a bow on top of the gift and handed it to me to place under the tree.

Our Christmas tree was a blue spruce my dad and I had cut a week before on our annual trek up Dry Fork Canyon. As usual, after getting it home in the back of our pickup truck, we'd had to cut nearly two feet off the tree to fit it in our living room. Once it was amputated to the right height it was placed in our ancient red and green stand. While Mom directed, Dad slid the tree back and forth in front of the living room window until it met her specifications; then it was secured with tie wire to a couple of nails driven into the floor on each side of the tree near the baseboard.

"Done," said Dad as he rubbed his hands together and cupped them around his nose. "Ah," he said as he inhaled the fragrant odor of spruce gum on his hands, "that's Christmas. Now all we need is snow." He stuck his thumb and finger together and pulled them slowly apart, watching the gum lift the skin of his thumb toward his finger.

There had been one brief snowstorm in mid-November, but within a day or two all the snow melted, even the snow that huddled in the shade of the trees in the orchard. Several times the skies looked threatening, but all that developed were a few squalls of rain. With the rain came mud in the hundred acres of orchard that surrounded our house. The orchard clung to the gentle slope of the foothills to the east of our home. On the west of the house, in the heavier soil, were the pears—Bartletts and moonglows. And the apples—red and golden delicious, Granny Smiths, and Jonathans. On the east, where it was sandier, Elberta and Hale havens peaches hugged the fence line. Next to the house were the cherries—Bings and Lamberts for eating, Vans for pollinating, and Queen Anns for pies.

The well-being of our family was tied inexorably to the well-being of the orchard. If the weather was kind and water was plentiful, we lived a life of relative prosperity. If we were cursed with late frosts and too little water, the harvest was poor and so was our family. This past year had been a good one. Our trees had produced an abundant crop, and due to a late frost in the northwest part of the country, there was competition for our fruit, driving the prices up.

My mother handed me the final gift, and I reached to place it with the others under the tree.

"Plug in the lights," she said as I straightened up. She flicked off the light switch, plunging the room into darkness as I probed for the plug. The multicolored lights from the tree bathed the walls and ceiling of our living room in their rosy glow.

Dad turned from where he had been standing at the window and looked at the tree. "Beautiful, just beautiful. Now where's the snow?"

"Worried?" asked Mom.

Dad shrugged his shoulders. "Oh, we've had late winters before, but if we don't get snow up in the hills, we're going to be in trouble by the end of the summer."

"Have faith, John. The snow will come."

Dad smiled as he crossed the room to my mother, the tree lights turning his undershirt into a harlequin's costume. He stood behind her chair and rubbed her shoulders. "Elizabeth," he said as he bent to kiss the top of her head, "I think you have enough faith for both of us."

The next morning a slow drizzle spread up the hillside behind the house. I crunched up the graveled driveway toward the main road, watching fingers of mist reach up from the dark soil of the orchard to caress the naked branches of the trees. A minute later my seven-year-old sister, Ginger, scurried after me, holding her pink umbrella over her head. As we waited together for the school bus on the paved road in front of our house, we watched the dark, low-hanging clouds scud lazily by.

It was still drizzling when we returned home from school that afternoon. I ran down the gravel driveway to the house, my coat pulled over my head to ward off the rain. Ginger hurried to try to keep up with me, holding her umbrella in front of her like a lance. The odor of baked bread pulled me through the back door and into the kitchen.

"Hang your coats up and come have a piece of hot bread and honey to warm you up," sang my mother from the kitchen table.

"Where's Dad?" I asked.

"He's gone into town to pick up a load of firewood for Uncle Gus." Mom handed each of us a slab of bread covered with melting butter and golden honey. "Gus's truck's having problems again." I bit into the bread, and steam covered my eyeglasses. "He'll be home soon."

"Why do we call him Uncle Gus?" asked Ginger as she pushed damp strands of hair from her face.

Mom shrugged, "I guess because he and Aunt Pauline were the first people to welcome us when we moved here."

"When did we move here?" Ginger ran her pink tongue across the honey on her bread.

"Just over a dozen years ago, when Rob was just a newborn and you weren't even thought of, Sweet Pea."

"Oh," she said as she nibbled at the crust of the slice of bread. "Why wasn't I thought of?"

Mom chuckled, "That's just an expression." She turned toward the window as we heard the sound of tires on the gravel. "Dad's home," she said smiling. She sawed another healthy slice of bread from the steaming loaf and was drizzling honey onto it as Dad burst through the back door. He removed his hat and shook the rain from it before he closed the kitchen door. Quickly he hung up his coat and rubbed his hands together as he walked to the kitchen sink.

Mom gave him a quick kiss on the cheek as he washed his hands under the running faucet. "Gus needs to have somebody who knows what he's doing look at that truck," he said. "I think he's got his carburetor so out of whack he's never going to get it running." He dried his hands on the kitchen towel looped through the handle of our refrigerator.

"When's supper?" he asked, taking a healthy bite from the slice of honey bread.

"About an hour and a half. It looks later than it is with the clouds so thick. Rob and Ginger just barely came in from school."

Dad took his glasses off and wiped them on the towel. "You kids have homework?"

I nodded my head.

"Better get on it if you want to watch that Bing Crosby Christmas show tonight."

I slid off the chair and retrieved my math book from where I'd laid it, just inside the kitchen door. The enticing odor of the Christmas tree caressed me as I walked through the living room and started up the stairway to the second floor. I threw my math book on my bed and stepped to the window. I could see across the orchard to where the smoke from Uncle Gus's chimney was drifting upward through the slate gray skies, and I could smell the mustiness of the drizzle. Sprawling on the bed, I opened my book and began solving the assigned problems. Little did I know that they would be the least of my worries before the week ended.

2

THE NEXT MORNING the clouds had lifted and an intense blue winter sky greeted us. The gravel driveway was crusted with frost, and the last drops of rain had gathered in frozen puddles at the side of the road. Ginger and I stood stomping our feet to keep them warm until the bus arrived. We were excited. Today was the final day of schoolwork before tomorrow's Christmas party and then nearly two whole weeks of vacation.

The bus pulled up in front of our house, and Mr. Fletcher pushed open the door. "Hop in, 'fore you freeze t'death," he said cheerfully. The bus seemed barely warmer than the outside world as we settled onto the worn brown seats. I folded my arms and put my hands into my armpits to try to keep them warm. Ginger and I were the first two to be picked up by Mr. Fletcher in his ancient yellow Bluebird school bus. Half an hour later a full bus labored onto the school grounds and disgorged its load. Ginger's elementary school and my junior high shared a common playground.

"See ya later," called my sister as she ran toward the open door of the school. I waved at her and hurried into the junior high school. The wooden floors had been freshly oiled over the weekend, and the odor mingled with that of the Christmas trees that decorated each of the rooms. Every one of my teachers had a test or assignment we had to finish before the Christmas vacation. The day passed quickly.

As we boarded the bus for home, I noticed wisps of clouds streaming like mares' tails over the eastern mountains. The wind had freshened, and I could smell the odor of rain in the air.

"'Bout ready for Christmas?" called out Mr. Fletcher to no one in particular as he closed the door of the bus.

By the time we arrived at our house the wind was blowing a mist of rain into our faces. As we scrunched down the driveway, Ginger asked me, "Do you think it's ever going to snow?"

I shrugged my shoulders, "Sometime, I guess."

"I like snow for Christmas."

"So do I, Ginger."

The winter wind whipped the raindrops against the window in my upstairs bedroom. The drops ran together and raced in tiny rivers down the pane. There was no homework to do, no books or papers stuffed inside my coat to keep them dry. I had a sudden rush of excitement as I thought once again that Christmas was nearly upon us. I wandered downstairs to the living room and inspected the gifts beneath the tree. Quietly I examined each of the wrapped boxes. Sap had dripped from a bruised branch onto the gold ribbon adorning the largest gift. It formed a glistening teardrop. I sniffed the woodsy odor of spruce as I shook the package gently. There was no sound from within. The feeling of anticipation rose within me.

School was shortened the following day. We drank punch and nibbled on cookies until the last bell rang and we ran rejoicing into the school yard, liberated for two whole weeks. The rain had let up, and the winter sun shone weakly through the frosty air.

Ginger and I crashed through the kitchen door as soon as we arrived home. Mom had just removed a pan of gingerbread men from the oven and was letting them cool on the stove top. "You two wash up," she said, "and I'll put you to work decorating these cookies."

"Can we eat one?" Ginger pled, as she stood sniffing the gingerbread.

Mom's forehead creased. "Well, they're for Uncle Gus and Aunt Pauline." Ginger's face fell. "But maybe you two can eat one, just one."

Eagerly we consumed the warm gingerbread.

After supper, wrapped like cocooned butterflies in our winter coats, scarves, and gloves, the four of us walked in the crystal moonlight to Uncle Gus's house. Dad carried the plate of cookies as we trudged single file along the edge of the road.

Even though Uncle Gus and Aunt Pauline had no children, their house was much bigger than ours. A cov-ered porch with its roof held up by several wooden columns ran across the front of the house, and lights burned brightly in most of the windows. A pine wreath hung on each of the pillars, and a matching wreath hung on the front door.

"Merry Christmas!" Father called out as he knocked briskly on the door.

Aunt Pauline threw open the door and invited us in. She was barely as tall as I but twice as wide. She was wearing her usual plaid shirt that hung over denim pants. Uncle Gus was sitting on the couch, and he unfolded like a scarecrow getting to his feet.

"Come in, come in," he beckoned. Jack Sprat ran through my mind.

Their Christmas tree stood in the corner of the living room, decorated with strings of popcorn and cranberries, with a marzipan ornament hanging from every branch. Dad handed Aunt Pauline the cookies, then stepped next to the fireplace, where he stood rubbing his hands together.

"I'm putting that load of wood to good use," said Gus.

"Feels mighty good," replied my dad.

"Well, just sit yourselves down," said Pauline.

"Can't," said Mom, "we've got things to get done. Tomorrow's Christmas Eve." She edged towards the door. "Merry Christmas to you both."

There was a feeling of goodwill and comfort as we hurried home in the moonlight toward a Christmas Eve that would change our lives forever.

3

I AWOKE THE NEXT MORNING to the mouth-watering odor of bacon and eggs. I hopped out of bed and looked out my second-story window toward Uncle Gus's house. The wind was gusting, and the branches of the cherry trees were scratching their fingernails on a slate gray sky. A thin wisp of smoke blew nearly horizontally from Gus's chimney. I pulled on my jeans and a T-shirt and hurried down to breakfast.

Ginger was already at the kitchen table wiping up the last of her egg yolk with a corner of toast. Dad was wearing his heavy jacket and pulling the earflaps down from his cap. "I think I better check the trees," he said as he pulled on his gloves. "I thought I saw deer in the orchard last night. I just want to make sure they aren't eating the bark on the trees. He opened the back door, and the wind slapped it open against the wall. "Sorry about that," he said as he tugged the door shut behind him.

After breakfast I retreated to my room to wrap the gifts I had purchased for my family. Always a procrastinator, I had left this chore to the last minute. I finished wrapping the gifts and placed them under the tree, then took time to shake each of the other presents. The day dragged on.

It was nearly noon before Dad came in from his inspection tour. He stripped off his muddy boots by the back door and carried them into the house. "Somebody get me a piece of newspaper."

Mom handed him one, and he placed his boots inside the back door on the paper. "Well?" she asked.

"Deer have been eating the ends of the branches on the peaches. I don't think they've done much damage, but it's still early in the season."

"I wonder why they're down so low." said Mom. "Usually it takes the snow to drive them down out of the hills. And heaven knows we haven't had much of that."

Dad hung up his coat. "Not much of a Christmas without snow."

The day continued to drag on. Ginger and I detoured

through the living room and past the Christmas gifts every chance we had. By late afternoon the clouds had lowered and a wind-driven rain was pummeling the house. Dad built a fire in the fireplace and plugged in the tree lights. Suddenly a bolt of lightning flashed outside the windows, followed by a crash of thunder. Ginger let out a little squeal and ran to Dad. A second flash was followed even more quickly by a louder explosion. The lights flickered and then went out.

"It's a good thing we were going to eat supper by candlelight," called my mother from the kitchen. We heard her fishing around in the junk drawer, and then in the dimness she lit the candles on the table. A hard rain continued to pound the house while we ate supper.

"You kids better scoot up to bed," said Dad, once the table was cleared. "If you're not asleep when Santa comes, he won't leave any presents."

We hurried up to our bedrooms as quickly as the darkened house permitted, and I climbed into my bed. The sheets were icy to the touch, and I shivered as I pulled the quilt up around my neck. Suddenly Ginger called from across the hall. "My bed's wet!"

Reluctantly I climbed out of my bed and made my way across the hall to Ginger's room. I could barely find her in the dark. She grabbed my hand and pulled me toward the foot of her bed. As I reached out to touch her quilt, a drop of water splattered on the back of my hand. Ginger's quilt was soaked.

"Dad," I called down the stairwell, "the roof's leaking." I heard Dad and Mom climbing the stairs and saw the dim light of a candle reflecting off the hall walls. As soon as they entered the room the flame illuminated a steady drip falling silently from the ceiling to the soaked spot on Ginger's quilt.

Dad pulled the bed away from the wall, and Mom took the candle to bring back dry sheets and a blanket. Dad brought a pot from the kitchen and placed it under the drip. In the candlelight it appeared as if everyone was moving in slow motion. The raindrops beat out a steady cadence as they plunked into the pot. Outside, the wind whipped the rain against the house.

After Ginger was tucked into bed, Mom and Dad crept back downstairs. After I had burrowed back under my quilt, I heard the kitchen door open and close. A few moments later the feeble beam of a flashlight shone through my window onto the ceiling of my room. Keeping the blanket wrapped around me, I sat up in bed and leaned over to the windowsill. I could see the flashlight beam shining up through the rain as Dad tried to spot where the roof was leaking. The light disappeared around the corner of the house but soon reappeared. By its dim glow I could see that Dad was carrying a ladder. A few moments later the top of the ladder appeared over the edge of the first-floor roof, just outside my window. The ladder shook from side to side until Dad's face appeared over the edge of the roof. Gingerly he made his way across the roof, shining the flashlight on the second-floor roof above my room and moving carefully along the rain-slick shingles.

He disappeared around the back of the house. I had just about decided to lie back down when I saw the flashlight beam again. Dad slipped and slid on the rain-soaked roof to the ladder. "Elizabeth," he called into the night, "I think I found the leak. I'm coming down to get a tarp out of the garage. I'm going to need your help handing me up some rocks to hold it down in this wind." He climbed over the edge of the roof onto the ladder, and blackness enveloped the roof again.

"Rob," Ginger called quietly from her bedroom, "I think I hear Santa Claus on the roof."

"Better get to sleep then," I whispered loudly back to her.

Dad appeared again over the edge of the roof, pushing a folded tarp in front of him. Apparently Mom was carrying rocks up the ladder because periodically he'd lean down and then place a couple of rocks on the tarp. At last he climbed back onto the lower roof, took the rocks off the canvas, and placed them against the wall just outside my window. He shined the flashlight back down the ladder. "Don't shine it in my eyes," Mom called out. A moment later she climbed onto the roof. She was wearing a pair of galoshes and her rain slicker.

"I'm going around to the other side," said Dad. Although they were trying to be quiet, I could hear them through my window. "I can climb up against the chimney onto the upper roof. When I get up there, I'll need you to hand me up the tarp, and then when I get it in place, I'll need those rocks to hold it down."

Mom nodded as she pulled her hands inside her slicker, trying to keep them warm. A few moments passed until I heard Dad's footsteps on the roof above my head. "Elizabeth," he said in a low voice, "hand me up the tarp."

Mom grabbed the folded tarp and handed it up to Dad. I could hear a slap-thumping in the wind as he unfolded the tarp and the wind caught it. There was considerable commotion, and then Dad called out, "Hand me up a couple of them rocks. This thing's flappin' like a sail."

Mom bent over to pick up two of the rocks; then I

heard a scraping sound followed by a cry from Dad as he slid off the upper roof. Mom straightened up just as Dad flew by, striking her on the shoulder with his foot. She fell backward, and the two of them toppled over the edge of the lower roof. Mom grabbed for the ladder and pulled it with her as she disappeared from sight.

Ginger whispered loudly from her room, "I think Santa Claus just left."

I waited for the sound of the kitchen door. All that greeted me was silence. Quickly I climbed out of bed and pulled my Keds onto my bare feet.

"Where ya' going?" Ginger asked as I started down the stairs.

"To check on Santa Claus," I called back. I grabbed my coat out of the closet and hurried out the kitchen door. The wind slapped my face with rain, and I was soaked instantly. The night was so dark I could barely make out the corner of the house. Cautiously I felt my way around the house until I nearly tripped over the ladder that was lying with its base against the house and the top resting on what I thought was a log. I moved hand over hand along the ladder until I found that it was resting on Dad. The flashlight was still in his hand, but it was not shining. I shook the flashlight, and a dim beam came on. I could see Mom lying on the other side of the ladder, blood streaming from her nose. Neither one was moving. I let out a scream and stood dancing in the rain.

After what seemed an eternity, I regained some composure, lifted the ladder off Dad, and ran back into the house. By the beam of the flashlight I located the phone and snatched the receiver off the cradle. "Number, please," came the night operator's voice.

"Wilma, this is Rob Henderson. Get an ambulance! Mom and Dad have fallen off the roof!" I screamed frantically.

"Are you at home?" she asked.

"Yes, yes! Hurry, they're both unconscious."

"Rob, are they outside in this rain?"

I was crying now, "Yes, and Mom's bleeding!"

"Rob, you listen to me. Go get some blankets and cover them up. The ambulance will be there in a jiffy." The line went dead.

"What's wrong, Rob?" called Ginger from the darkness at the top of the stairs.

"Just go back to bed, Ginger," I commanded. The flashlight went out. I searched in the darkness for the linen closet in the hall, found it, and dragged out two wool blankets. Back into the rain I went. A distant flash of lightning revealed my parents lying as I had left them. Blood continued to stream from Mom's nose, and the pool of water under her head was tinted pink. Another flash revealed Dad's left leg twisted at an unnatural angle. I spread the blankets over the two of them, but the wind picked up the corners of the quilts and swirled them into sodden ropes. I fought to keep the blankets in place. After what seemed a long time, in the distance I could hear the faint sound of a siren.

A few minutes later the ambulance pulled into the driveway, and I could see the flashes of red light pulsing off the trees in the orchard. I screamed against the wind, and two men in yellow rain slickers raced around the corner of the house, their powerful flashlights piercing the darkness. They knelt beside Mom and Dad and searched for a pulse. One of the men turned to me. I recognized Tom Ambrose's voice. "Rob, you scoot in the house and get into some dry clothes. We'll take care of your Mom and Dad."

The other man had run back around the house, and a moment later he backed the ambulance right across our front lawn and close to where Mom and Dad lay. Another car with flashing emergency lights pulled into the driveway. Deputy Sheriff Parker came running around the side of the house. He and Tom talked for a moment, then he helped lift Mom and Dad onto the stretchers the ambulance carried. After lifting the stretchers into the back of the ambulance, Tom Ambrose climbed inside, and Deputy Parker slammed the door closed. The driver drove back onto the road, and the siren began wailing as they sped off into the rain-washed night.

Deputy Parker led me back into the house. "You get into something dry, you hear?" I nodded my head. "Is there anyone you could call to come over and spend the night with you?"

I shrugged my shoulders. I was shivering badly now, partly from the rain and cold and partly from seeing my parents carried off in an ambulance. "Where are they taking Mom and Dad?"

"They're on their way to the clinic. You can visit them in the morning. Right now I'm concerned about someone staying with you kids the rest of the night."

"We'll be okay," I chattered. "We don't need to bother anyone. It's Christmas Eve."

Deputy Parker shook his head. "Either we find somebody to come stay with you or I'll bundle the two of you up and have you stay with my wife and me."

Somehow I felt a welling within me, and I knew I didn't want to leave the safety of our home. "I guess we could call Aunt Pauline," I ventured.

"What's her number?"

I knew their number like my own, but at that minute I couldn't for the life of me remember it. "Wilma's running the switchboard; she'll know it," I finally said.

Deputy Parker lifted the receiver. "Wilma, this is Pat Parker. I need to talk to Gus and Pauline Rogers." He paused a moment, "Thanks."

I stood shaking so hard I looked like a wet puppy.

"Pauline, this is Pat Parker. There's been an accident at the Hendersons'. I wonder if you could come over and take care of the kids." I could hear Aunt Pauline's voice in panic on the phone. "Well, it seems like John and Elizabeth fell off the roof." He paused again and pieces of Aunt Pauline's voice questioned further. "Don't really know, but I know we need somebody to come spend the night with the kids." He turned his flashlight on me and saw me standing in a widening pool of water. He covered the mouthpiece of the receiver. "Get upstairs and get some dry clothes on," he ordered. Then back into the receiver. "Much obliged." He hung up.

By the time Aunt Pauline arrived, I had toweled off and put on my other pair of pajamas. She and Deputy Parker spoke in hushed tones for a few minutes and then he left. Aunt Pauline shook the rain from her slicker and hung it in the hall closet; then she and I sat on the couch in the darkness of the front room. The silhouette of the

Christmas tree was barely visible against the window. "How soon can we go see Mom and Dad?"

She shook her head. "They'll be all right. Now, you need to get into bed and get some sleep," she whispered. "I can't believe your sister slept through all of this." Just then the lights came back on.

4

CHRISTMAS MORNING dawned gray and sodden. The rain and wind continued to beat on the house like waves on the shore. I had not thought I had slept after I crawled back into bed, but I must have drifted off into a troubled sleep because Ginger was shaking me awake.

"It's Christmas," she said, the excitement in her voice as tangible as the odor of a fire in the hearth. "Let's go see what Santa brought!" She was dancing around my bed.

I heard the heavy tread of Aunt Pauline climbing the stairs. She stuck her head though the doorway into my room. Just then the phone rang. "I'll get it," I said as I jumped from my bed, raced down the stairs to the kitchen, and grabbed the phone.

"Hello?"

"Rob?" All sorts of feelings mixed within me. It was Mom.

"Mom. Are you all right?"

"Stiff and sore, but I'll be fine. Are you two there alone?"

"Aunt Pauline's here too."

"Oh, good. Let me talk to her."

"Aunt Pauline, Mom wants to talk to you," I called up the stairs.

"Oh, thank heaven," said Aunt Pauline as she clumped down the stairs. I handed her the phone. "Elizabeth, is everything all right?"

Aunt Pauline sat down on one of our kitchen chairs. Ginger came down the stairs into the kitchen. "Why's Aunt Pauline here?" she asked. "Where are Mom and Dad?"

"They fell off the roof last night," I said. "They're over at the clinic."

Ginger's eyes grew wide. "Were they trying to catch Santa Claus?"

I shook my head. "They were trying to fix the leaking roof."

"Sure, right away," said Aunt Pauline into the phone. "Be there as soon as we can." She reached and hung up the phone.

"You two hurry up and get dressed. I'm going to call Gus and get him to bring the car over here so we can go to the hospital."

"Hospital? I thought they were at the clinic," I said. In my mind there was a world of difference. The clinic in our little community was where you went for a checkup or to get shots; the hospital was in the next town and implied surgery or worse.

"Your folks are at the hospital. Now scat and get dressed." She turned to the phone again and jiggled the cradle. "Joyce, is that you? Give me 1001. This is Pauline; I need to talk to Gus."

Ginger and I climbed back up the stairs to get dressed. "When are we gonna open our presents?" she pouted.

"After we go get Mom and Dad," I replied. "Now hurry."

The two of us pulled on our clothing and hurried back down to the kitchen. "Your Uncle Gus is on his way," she said. "Make sure you bundle up against the rain." She retrieved her slicker from the front hall closet, and Ginger and I both hurried through the kitchen and pulled our coats off the coat hangers near the back door.

Just then we heard a car pull into the driveway. I could see the top of Uncle Gus's pea-green and white, two-toned Hudson Hornet through the kitchen window.

"Come on, you two," called Aunt Pauline. "Let's go see your folks."

We hurried out the kitchen door and crunched quickly on the rain-soaked gravel to the car. We climbed into the backseat while Aunt Pauline hopped in next to Uncle Gus.

"It's a dirty shame," said Uncle Gus, "just a dirty shame. And on Christmas to boot."

"Shhh," whispered Aunt Pauline, and I saw her glance at the two of us in the backseat.

Uncle Gus backed the car onto the highway and started toward town. The windshield wipers barely kept ahead of the rain as we crept down the road. There was no other traffic, and we passed no one going in either direction. It was as if, at that moment, we were isolated from the rest of the world—a world wrapped in tinsel and pine boughs and presents left beneath the Christmas tree, while we sloshed slowly down a forsaken highway toward the hospital where my mother and father waited for us.

The hospital was nearly thirty miles away, and it took us almost an hour to arrive. Uncle Gus pulled the

Hudson up to the front door, and his three passengers bowed their heads against the rain and pushed through the double doors while he parked the car.

The foyer was completely empty except for an old, old woman who sat behind a counter. A Christmas tree decorated with paper angels and golden tinsel stood beside the door. "May I help you?" the old woman's voice crackled across the room.

"We're looking for John and Elizabeth Henderson," said Aunt Pauline. "They were brought in last night. They fell off their roof . . ." she trailed off.

The old woman searched for a moment. It was so quiet I could hear the sound of her finger scratching down the sheet of paper. "Here they are," she said brightly, "Room 204. The elevator's right around the corner," she pointed.

"Thank you," said Aunt Pauline. Just then Uncle Gus burst through the door and shook the rain from his coat.

"You're welcome," said the old woman, "and Merry Christmas."

The four of us rounded the corner, and Aunt Pauline punched the up button on the elevator. We could hear the groanings of ancient machinery before the door slid open and we entered. Mom was waiting as the elevator doors opened on the second floor. She had strips of adhesive tape across the bridge of her nose, and bruises darkened both of her eyes. A sling supported her left arm. Ginger started to cry.

Mom dropped slowly to her knees and put her right arm around Ginger. "It's all right, Baby," she said, patting her on her back. Ginger burrowed into Mom's shoulder. I saw Mom wince.

"Helluva Christmas present," growled Uncle Gus as he stepped behind me and wrapped his arms around me.

"Where's Dad?" I asked timidly. Mom stood slowly and took hold of Ginger's hand.

"He's in his room," she said tilting her head down the hallway.

"How is he?" Aunt Pauline asked warily.

Mom turned slowly and looked out the window at the clouds swollen with rain. "He'll be fine," she said firmly in a low voice. She turned back to Aunt Pauline. "He'll be just fine."

From somewhere in the hospital a chime sounded twice. We walked past the nurses' station toward Dad's room. Mom limped slightly. "And how are you?" asked Aunt Pauline.

"I'm fine," replied Mom in hushed tones.

"Meaning what?"

"Nothing important," replied Mom. "Broken nose, broken wrist, but I'm fine."

The blinds had been closed in Dad's room, and a single night-light gave off its feeble glow above the washstand next to his bed. Dad lay in bed with his left leg encased in plaster and supported in a sling that hung from a steel frame above the foot of his bed. A plastic tube ran from a bottle above his head into the back of his left hand. But most frightening, his head was swathed in bandages. His cheek was raw and I could see the cat whiskers of stitches just below his cheekbone. I felt tears well up in my eyes.

"Has he come to?" asked Uncle Gus.

Mom shook her head, "Not yet . . . but he will." She sat down in the chair by the side of the bed and reached out her good hand to stroke the back of Dad's hand. "He will," she repeated.

A large woman in a white nurse's uniform pushed open the door to Dad's room. "Only two visitors at a time," she said. "And children under twelve aren't allowed."

Aunt Pauline and Uncle Gus led Ginger out into the hallway. The nurse stuck a thermometer into Dad's mouth and unrolled the gray tongue of the blood pressure cuff. With a quiet efficiency she squeezed the bulb to inflate the band around Dad's arm. She stuffed the stethoscope into her ears, and I could hear the quiet "whish" of air as she released the thumb screw and deflated the cuff.

Once she had finished writing the results on a clipboard that hung on the bottom of the bed she turned to Mom. "You might as well go home; there's nothing you can do here, and you look like you could use some sleep. We'll call if there's any change."

"How is he?" asked Mom.

"As well as can be expected. He took a nasty fall." She pursed her lips. "Honey, it's going to take a while. Just go on home and we'll call."

Reluctantly we coaxed Mom into coming home with us. We had not thought to bring her a coat, so Uncle Gus gave her his, then went into the parking lot and started the car. He turned the heater on high in the Hudson. Aunt Pauline insisted that Mom ride in the front seat, closer to the heater. From the backseat I could see Mom shivering, even though the car was warm enough that I struggled out of my coat. Ginger sat next to me sucking on the knuckle of her hand.

The rain continued to splat against the windshield, but partway home it began to leave little feathery tails on the glass, and by the time we arrived at our house the rain had turned to snow.

5

"ARE YOU SURE YOU'RE going to be all right?"
asked Aunt Pauline as we pulled into our driveway.
"Would you like me to stay here and help?"

"We'll be fine," Mom said wearily as we climbed out
of the car. "Thanks for all you've done." The snow
swirled around us as the three of us climbed the porch
steps and opened the front door of our house and the
Hudson pulled away.

Ginger and I hung our coats on the pegs near the
kitchen door and hurried into the front room. "Rob,
would you plug in the lights on the Christmas tree,
please," said Mom as she sank onto the couch.

I plugged in the lights. Despite the trauma our family

had felt, despite Mom sitting forlornly on the couch with her face taped and her arm in a sling, despite the silent trip home in Uncle Gus's Hudson, the Christmas tree reached out with the eternal hope of the season and enveloped the three of us in its warmth. Through the window behind the tree we could see the snowflakes falling silently and softly on the orchard.

"Mom, is Dad going to be all right?" asked Ginger almost in a whisper, as she pulled herself into the rocking chair.

Mom nodded her head. "He's going to be just fine, Sweet Pea." She rose painfully from the couch and walked to the Christmas tree, then reached out and touched an ornament gently. "He'll be just fine."

I thought of Dad lying in his hospital bed, head swathed in bandages, a tube hooked into his hand, and then looked at Mom standing by the Christmas tree, looking out the window. I couldn't help it, and at that moment tears swelled in my eyes and ran down my cheeks.

Ginger slid off the rocking chair and went to Mom. She clutched Mom's skirt and gently tugged on it. "When are we going to open our presents?"

My mother and father were of one mind on many issues but not when it came to wrapping Christmas gifts.

Dad came from a family that never wrapped gifts, Mom from a family that always did. The compromise they had reached was simply that Mom wrapped all the gifts, and Dad complained about it. Thus, a tantalizing assortment of carefully wrapped boxes was mounded around the base of the Christmas tree.

"I have an idea," said Mom. "Why don't we wait until Dad comes home to have our Christmas? What do you think?"

"Will he be home later?" asked Ginger.

"Yes, Sweet Pea. But maybe not today."

I joined my mother and sister at the Christmas tree. "I think that's a good idea," I said softly as I wiped the tears from my cheeks. The three of us stood gazing at the snowflakes falling on the orchard. The ground was already covered, and the dark branches of the trees stood like church spires, pointing toward God in his heaven.

"Rob, would you go out and put that thing away?" asked Mom as she pointed to the ladder lying where it had fallen last night.

I slipped on my coat, opened the kitchen door, and made my way around the corner of the house. The ladder was already covered with snow. I picked it up and carried it back to the shed where Dad kept his tools. After wrestling with it for a few minutes, I was able to lift it onto the wall brackets in the shed. The shed had a distinctive odor—a mixture of oil and leather and freshly cut wood. It brought back such powerful memories of my father that I sat down on a sawhorse and wept. In my despair I called out, "Heavenly Father, please make him well. Please, bring Dad home." Deep within me a well of self-pity and loneliness filled drop by drop as I sat in the stillness of my father's sanctuary.

Through the open door of the shed I could see the snowflakes falling. I could see the puffs of my breath forming tiny clouds of fog as I tried to find comfort in the memories of my father.

6

AN HOUR LATER I WAS gamely trying to fix a Christmas dinner for us under Mom's direction. I was fairly adept at tuna fish sandwiches but had no idea how to cook a Christmas ham. Slowly, while I chewed on my tongue, I used a knife to score the surface of the ham into tiny diamonds and then place a clove in the center of each one. Then Mom coached me on how to arrange slices of pineapple on top and pour the juice over the ham. Mom turned on the oven, and I placed my masterpiece inside. Just then the phone rang. Mom snatched the receiver from its cradle.

"Hello," she said with a mixture of anxiety and hope in her voice. "Oh, Pauline. No, we haven't heard anything. I thought I'd go back over to the hospital in a few minutes." She reached out with her foot and pulled a chair over next to the phone, then carefully sat down.

"I'm sure I can do just fine." She glanced down at her arm in a cast. "I wouldn't think of putting you out." Her shoulders sagged a little. "Well, if you insist. One o'clock will be fine. Thanks, Pauline. Good-bye."

Mom hung up the phone. "Pauline and Gus are going to drive me over to the hospital." She raised her arm in the sling slightly. "I'm beginning to feel pretty helpless."

I could hear Ginger shaking the Christmas presents that were still carefully wrapped and lying beneath the tree. "I won't be too long. Will you and your sister be okay?" I nodded my head.

An hour later, potatoes had been peeled and put on to boil, and the delicious odor of the baking ham filled the kitchen. I saw Mom looking anxiously at the clock. At noon we ate our Christmas feast. My first experience at carving a ham was less than perfect, but it tasted good, just the same. The hands on the clock continued to crawl slowly toward one o'clock.

Ginger and I were washing and drying the dishes when I heard a car pull up in the driveway. I helped Mom drape her coat over her shoulders. "Ginger, Rob's in charge. I'll be back soon. I'm going to see your dad."

"Is he going to come home?" she asked.

"Maybe not today, Sweet Pea. We'll just have to wait and see."

Uncle Gus honked the horn and Mom walked out the front door, across the porch, and carefully down the front steps. Nearly six inches of snow had fallen. Mom turned back to the two of us standing in the open doorway. "Can you get that snow off the steps, Rob?" she asked.

I nodded my head. Mom climbed into the front seat next to Uncle Gus. Aunt Pauline rolled down the back window and waved as the car backed out of the driveway. Ginger and I went back into the house.

"Rob, why's Mom so sad?" asked my sister.

I shrugged my shoulders. "Just worried about Dad, I guess."

"What if he doesn't come home today? Will we . . ." she left the rest of the sentence hanging.

"Then I guess he'll come home tomorrow, or the next day."

Ginger's eyes turned to the presents under the tree. "I hope he comes home soon," she said.

I turned on the radio, and Christmas music flooded the front room. "Want me to read you a story?" I asked.

"Guess so."

"You pick one, and I'll read it to you."

I heard Ginger's footsteps as she climbed the stairs to her bedroom.

"Rob, Rob, hurry!"

I raced up the stairs to her room. The slow drip of the previous evening had continued, and the pot on the floor had filled to overflowing. I carried it to the bathroom and dumped it in the toilet, then returned it to Ginger's room. We had a stack of old diapers stored in the cabinet near our washing machine. I hurried downstairs, retrieved one, and returned to my sister's room to mop up the water.

"I think the snow's going to freeze, and the drip will stop until it thaws," I said. Ginger nodded her head. "Now pick a book, and we'll go read it."

Ginger touched each of the books on the shelf beneath her window. "How about this one?" she said, pulling *The Magic of Oz* from the shelf. "I like the part about the monkeys."

Together we descended the stairs of our empty house. The lights on the tree still shined brightly, and the presents beckoned from beneath the tree, but the house was still, very still. The snow continued to fall, and the skies were dark. I turned on the table lamp, and the two of us settled on the couch. Ginger opened the book, and I began to read, "On the east edge of the Land of Oz, in the Munchkin Country, is a big, tall hill called Mount Munch . . ."

We had barely finished a chapter when I felt my sister's head fall against my arm. As gently as I could, I lowered her head to the couch and then lifted her feet into place. I pulled the afghan off the back of the couch and spread it over her, then turned the radio down so the Christmas carols played softly in the background.

I went into the kitchen and pulled a strip of meat from the ham in the refrigerator and munched on it as I looked at the snow piling up in the orchard. My coat hung near the kitchen door. I put it on, wrapped a scarf around my neck and ears, and searched in vain for my gloves. Then I got the snow shovel from the shed and shuffled down the driveway to the front of the house, creating two deep furrows in the snow. The steps were broad, and it took nearly half an hour to clear them and the porch of the heavy, wet snow.

Ginger was still asleep when I let myself in through the kitchen door and hung up my coat. The Christmas music was still playing as quietly as a lullaby. I climbed the stairs to Ginger's room and checked the leaking roof. The drip had stopped, but with Dad in the hospital, I wondered who was going to fix the roof, and a flood of loneliness overwhelmed me again. I returned to the front room, where Ginger slept soundly. I slid into Mom's rocking chair, pulled my feet up, and rested my chin on my knees. Outside, daylight was fading while the snow continued to fall. Even with the lights on the Christmas tree glowing in the gathering darkness, the house seemed cold and empty. Suddenly I realized that no one had shoveled coal into the furnace stoker all day.

The basement with its single electric light smelled of coal dust. I pulled open the creaking door of the furnace and was relieved to see the fire had not gone out. I opened the top of the stoker. It was nearly empty. The coal pile was near the chute on the east wall. I picked up Dad's big shovel and began filling the stoker. Without warning the stoker worm drive began turning, delivering coal to the furnace, and the flickering fire behind the furnace grate suddenly sprang to life. After shoveling in a few more scoops of coal, I hurried back upstairs.

After washing the coal dust off my hands, I tiptoed back into the front room. The Christmas music had been replaced by news, and I was reaching to turn off the radio when the announcer said, "County crews are working as fast as they can to plow and sand the roads; however, anyone who does not have an emergency should stay home. The police department has advised us that all personnel are involved in investigating the scores of accidents that have been caused by the slick roads. The earlier rain has frozen beneath the snow, and even after plowing, black ice may remain. If you have been involved in an accident and are listening on your car radio, please be advised that it may be some time before an investigating officer can get to you. We now return you to twenty-four hours of Christmas carols on KWAK, your station for continuous music."

Ginger was still asleep on the couch. The clock said ten minutes until six. Mom had been gone nearly five hours. A growing certainty rose in my chest: I knew that Mom had been in an accident and that she, Uncle Gus, and Aunt Pauline were somewhere off the road between here and the hospital. Near panic, I snatched the phone off the hook.

"Number, please," came the disembodied voice.

"Joyce?" I asked.

"This is Maxine. Can I help you?"

"This is Rob Henderson. I was wondering—"

"Oh, Rob, how are your folks? Joyce told me what happened when I came on shift."

"That's the problem. Mom went over to the hospital to visit Dad, and she should have been home hours ago." My voice was rising in pitch.

"Let me check with the sheriff, and I'll call you right back." The line went dead.

I put the phone back in its cradle and stared at it, willing it to ring. I could hear Ginger stirring in the front room. "Rob," she called out.

"In the kitchen," I replied. She came through the door rubbing her eyes with the backs of her fists.

"Where's Mom?"

Just then the phone rang. Even though I was waiting for the call, it startled me. I plucked the receiver from its cradle, "Hello?"

"Rob, this is Maxine. The dispatcher says he hasn't heard anything about your mother, but they've got nearly a dozen accidents they haven't gotten to yet. If I hear anything, I'll give you a call."

"Thanks," I managed to squeak.

"What's the matter, Rob?" asked my sister.

"Nothing," I barked too quickly. "Are you hungry?" Ginger nodded her head. "Want a ham sandwich?" She nodded her head again.

"When's Mom going to be home?" she asked.

"Soon. Get a loaf of bread out of the bread box." Ginger opened the bread box and removed one of the loaves that Mom had baked on the last day of school. That seemed like weeks ago. I sliced the bread as evenly as I could, then cut off some of the ham. Ginger got some milk and a bottle of pickles out of the refrigerator, and we ate our ham sandwiches and drank our milk in silence.

"Rob, what's wrong?"

"Nothing," I said quickly, "nothing at all. I'd better go shovel the front steps again so Mom won't slip when she gets home."

I put my coat on, turned on the front porch light, and went out the front door. I'd left the snow shovel leaning against the front of the house, and only an inch or so of snow had accumulated since I'd last cleared the steps. This snow was light and fluffy and easy to shovel. I was just finishing the bottom step when I saw headlights turn into our driveway, and I stood staring as Uncle Gus's Hudson stopped and Mom climbed out of the car.

I felt such relief that my knees felt weak.

"Thanks, so much," she said as she pushed the door closed with her good hand, then shuffled through the deep snow to the porch steps.

"Hi, Mom. How's Dad?" I tried to sound unconcerned.

"Where are your gloves?" she asked. "You'll freeze your hands to death."

I shoveled the last scoop from the step and shrugged.

"I couldn't find them. Maybe I left them in my locker at school."

Mom's eyes were red. She reached out her hand and put it on my shoulder, "I'm sorry I barked at you, Rob. I'm really tired. It hasn't been the best day." She climbed the steps wearily.

"How's Dad?" I asked again.

"Not much change," she said. "They said the next seventy-two hours are going to be the test. If he doesn't wake up . . ." Her voice trailed off and her shoulders slumped.

"Then what?" I whispered.

Mom's shoulders straightened, and she steadied herself against the door handle. "He will wake up, Rob. I know he will." She opened the door and walked into the house.

7

THE SNOW CONTINUED to fall through the night. When we arose the next morning, another six inches lay on the front steps. Thankfully it was light and fluffy and could be pushed off without too much trouble. I finished cleaning the front steps, then cleared off the stairs leading to the back door. When I pushed open the kitchen door and stomped the snow off my feet, Mom was at the stove scrambling eggs with her good hand.

"Rob, would you check the stoker? The furnace isn't putting out much heat."

I remembered that I had shoveled only a couple of scoops into the stoker last night. As I clumped down the basement stairs I could feel a chill in the air. The furnace had gone out.

"Mom," I called up the stairs, "the fire's out."

"Get the clinkers out before you start it again," she said matter-of-factly.

The bottom of the firebox was covered with hard, brown, lava-like remnants of the burned coal. I used the furnace tongs to remove them one by one through the open door. As I dropped them clattering into the metal washtubs we kept near the furnace, I wondered, with Dad gone, who was going to haul them up the steps.

Although Dad didn't seem to mind starting a fire in the furnace, I hated it. First, newspaper was balled up and placed in the bottom of the chamber. Then sticks of kindling were placed on top of the newspaper, followed by some small chunks of coal. I could never do this without getting soot all over my hands and arms and often on my face. A box of kitchen matches lay on the sill of the small window near the ceiling. I struck a match and lit the newspaper. It began to burn brightly, and I watched as the flames licked at the kindling. The door of the furnace had a sliding damper to regulate the amount of air reaching the conflagration inside. I opened the damper wide and closed the door. Curls of smoke escaped through the open slats as the fire began to take hold.

I opened the top of the stoker box and began shoveling coal into it. It took Dad twenty-four scoops of coal to fill the stoker. I knew that because I had counted them when I watched him fill the hopper. I tried to shovel just as much coal as he did, but it took me forty scoops. Even in the coldness of the cellar, sweat trickled down my back. Coal dust filled the basement and swirled in tiny eddies as it met the current of heat coming from the furnace. At last I heard the worm drive of the stoker turn on and begin feeding coal into the furnace. At least my fire building had been successful. I climbed back upstairs to the kitchen.

"Go wash your hands, and I'll have some ham and eggs ready for you," Mom said with feigned cheerfulness.

While I was washing my hands, Ginger pounded on the bathroom door. "Hurry, Rob, I gotta go."

She pushed past me in her pajamas as I exited the bathroom. A few minutes later the two of us sat down at the kitchen table. Mom scooped eggs and fried ham out of the frying pan onto our plates and then carried them one at a time to the table.

"Is Daddy coming home today?" Ginger asked.

I saw Mom blink rapidly, "I hope so, Sweet Pea." Mom rose from the table and went to the sink. The last flakes of snow pirouetted past the kitchen window. She stared, unseeing, at the quilted surface of the orchard, each square stitched with a tree trunk at its corners.

"Eat your breakfast," I said quietly to Ginger. "Dad will come home when he's ready."

"I hope it's soon."

"So do I," said Mom softly from her silent station at the sink.

After breakfast was finished and the dishes washed, I tugged on my coat and went out on the front porch to shovel the last remnants of snow from the steps. While I was doing so, Uncle Gus pulled into the driveway and unfolded from his car.

"Mornin', Rob," he said cheerfully. Uncle Gus was dressed, as he usually was, in a pair of blue-and-white striped overalls. They always looked too big for his skinny frame. A fleece-lined coat hung uncertainly on his shoulders. He had the ear flaps on his aviator cap pulled down over his ears. The only thing that looked out of place was the pair of shiny, black leather gloves on his hands.

"Is your mom here?" he asked as he walked toward the front steps.

I nodded. "She's in the kitchen."

He pulled off the gloves, "My Christmas present," he said turning them over in his hands. "Driving gloves," he said, as if he needed to explain. He took the front steps two at a time and opened the front door. "Anybody home?" he called through the open door.

I propped the snow shovel against the porch railing and sought the warmth of the house. Mom and Uncle Gus were talking as I took my coat off and hung it on its accustomed peg near the kitchen door.

"Gus, I just can't have you spending all your time driving me to the hospital."

"Nonsense," he replied, "there's no way you can hold onto the steering wheel and shift with that broken wrist. Besides, that's what friends are for."

"But I can't expect you to drop everything and—"

"Elizabeth," he said shaking his head, "there's not much I can do in my orchard with all this snow. Now, get your coat and get in the car. If the kids need anything, they can call Pauline."

"At least let me pay you for the gasoline," she replied.

"Don't you worry about that," he said. "Now dress warm; it's pretty cold out there." He gestured at the kitchen window. "Besides, it'll give me a chance to use these new driving gloves Pauline gave me for Christmas." He chuckled softly.

"Mom," said Ginger, "are you going again?"

My mother dropped slowly to her knees next to Ginger's chair. "I'm going to see your dad."

"Is he coming home today?"

"I don't know, Ginger, but I hope so."

Ginger slipped off her chair and hugged Mom. I could see the flicker of pain in my mother's eyes as Ginger squeezed her. "Bring him home," she said as she buried her face in Mom's shoulder.

Mom pushed heavily on the edge of the table with her good hand as she rose to her feet. "Will you be okay, Rob?"

I nodded my head. "Sure."

A few minutes later, Mom and Uncle Gus walked carefully down the front steps. Uncle Gus held Mom's right elbow and helped her to the car. I watched through the window as they backed out of the driveway and disappeared down the road.

Ginger was sitting on the living room floor gently shaking a Christmas present wrapped in red foil and decorated with a gold ribbon. "I wonder what's in here," she said as she raised it to her ear.

"I don't know, Ginger, but I hope we get to open them soon."

"So do I, Rob."

CAN WE MAKE A snowman?" my sister asked.

The snow had stopped, and the clouds were thinning.

There wasn't anything else to do, so I said, "Sure. Put on your snowsuit and galoshes." I put on my coat and searched again for my gloves. I finally found them stuffed behind my school books on the sideboard.

The snow was too fluffy to pack easily, and we tried unsuccessfully to roll snowballs to make a snowman. We ended up dropping on our backs into the powder and moving our arms to make snow angels. The clouds streamed by overhead so that it felt as if the world were turning beneath us.

Ginger rolled onto her side. "When's Mom coming home?"

I lay watching the clouds disappear over the mountain.

"Pretty soon, I guess."

"Do you think her arm hurts?"

I thought of Mom wincing when Ginger squeezed her. "Probably."

"Are you mad at Dad?"

"Mad? No, why would you ask that?"

"Well, we were supposed to open our presents. I mean, we would have if he was home," my sister said solemnly.

I could feel the coldness of the snow seeping through the warmth of my coat.

"Hungry?" I asked.

"Sort of," answered Ginger.

"Let's go in the house, and I'll fix you some lunch."

The two of us climbed the back steps and brushed as much snow from our coats as we could before we entered the kitchen. The warmth of the kitchen surrounded us, and the odor of fried ham lingered in the air. The furnace hummed and clunked in the basement.

While I was fixing lunch Ginger turned on the television set, and we ate our sandwiches in the living room, where we watched the *Kukla, Fran, and Ollie Show.* We had a Hoffman television set with a yellow glass over the small screen. I fiddled with the rabbit ears, but the picture still wasn't very clear. After we finished eating, I took our lunch plates into the kitchen and washed them while Ginger curled up on the couch and continued watching the show.

Through the kitchen window I could see clouds had gathered again and a new batch of snowflakes was beginning to fall. I returned to the front room to find that Ginger had fallen asleep. I turned off the television, plugged in the Christmas tree lights, and sat in the rocking chair. The chair squeaked softly as I rocked back and forth, thinking. The enormity of Dad's accident began to weigh on me. Like a flock of quail, a dozen questions fluttered around in my mind. Who will keep the deer out of the orchard? Who will prune the trees? Who will take our watering turns? It's bad enough to have to keep the stoker filled and the steps shoveled, but, worst of all, who will move the bees into the orchard?

There were many things in this world that frightened me, but bees absolutely terrified me. The sound of their buzzing sent me running for cover. One of the distinctive memories I had from my early childhood was being stung by a bee on my cheek and having it swell until I could barely open my eye.

The questions continued to flash in my mind as the clouds thickened and darkness surrounded and enveloped our house. The only lights were those on the tree, and the gifts beneath the tree reflected the diffused colors of the rainbow. *When will Mom get home?* I wondered. She's been gone for hours. I slid out of the rocking chair and turned on the front porch light. Ginger continued to sleep soundly on the couch. I stood at the front window and peered down the road. Few cars were passing on the paved road, but when they did their lights shone through the scattering of snow that continued to fall.

The telephone rang, startling me. I ran into the kitchen and grabbed the receiver.

"Hello?"

"Rob, this is Aunt Pauline. You haven't seen Gus, have you?"

"Not since he left to go to the hospital this morning," I replied.

"I thought they'd be back by now. Are you kids all right?"

"We're fine," I said.

Ginger flipped on the kitchen light. I squinted in the sudden brightness.

"Who's on the phone?" she asked.

I covered the mouthpiece, "Aunt Pauline," I mouthed.

"When's Uncle Gus bringing Mom home?"

"Soon."

Aunt Pauline had said something, but I hadn't heard. I uncovered the mouthpiece. "I'm sorry, what was that?"

"I said, you send Gus packing as soon as he gets your mom home."

"We will."

"What are you two having for supper?"

"I dunno," I replied.

There was a slight pause. "You have Gus bring you all over here," she said.

I heard the crunch of wheels on the snow and gravel of our driveway. "I think they just got here. Let me check." I put down the receiver and hurried into the front room. I could see Uncle Gus's Hudson in the front porch light. I scurried back to the phone.

"They're here," I said.

"Well, you all hurry right over."

I hung up the phone and turned to Ginger. "Get your snowsuit on, we're going over to Aunt Pauline's for supper."

My coat and Ginger's snowsuit were still damp from our earlier excursion, but we were putting them on just as Mom and Uncle Gus came through the front door. Uncle Gus was helping support Mom by holding the elbow of her good arm.

"I'm sure everything will work out," he said.

Mom's eyes looked red, but I wasn't sure if it was from the Christmas lights or not. "Yes, it will," she said firmly. "Thanks, Gus, for hauling me all the way over to the hospital and back."

He patted her on the shoulder. "That's what neighbors are for."

Ginger ran to Mom and wrapped her arms around her legs. "I'm glad you're home," she said into our mother's skirt.

"I'm glad to be home."

"Mom, Aunt Pauline invited us for supper," I said, buttoning up my coat. "If that's all right, I mean."

Uncle Gus smiled his toothy smile. "Everybody out to the car. Don't forget to unplug the lights."

Aunt Pauline was busy in the kitchen when we entered the house. The odor of baking bread mingled with the peppery smell of stew simmering on the stove. She wiped her hands on her apron, "I was getting worried."

"I'm sorry to have kept your husband at the hospital so long," stammered my mother.

Aunt Pauline waved her hand in dismissal, "Oh, don't worry about that. I was just afraid something might have happened on these slick roads."

"Now, Pauline," said Uncle Gus, "you know I'm a better driver than that." He smiled a tight little smile.

"I wasn't questioning your driving ability," she replied. "Now, sit down and let's have some supper."

Ginger and I looked for a place to put our coat and snowsuit. Finally we laid them on the couch in the living room and hurried into the dining room. Aunt Pauline had placed a basket of rolls on the table and was carrying the pot of stew from the kitchen. "It's not much," she said, "but I think it will fill you up."

I realized how hungry I was as Uncle Gus filled my bowl with steaming stew and passed it to me.

"How is he?" asked Aunt Pauline once we were all ladling stew into our mouths.

"About the same," my mother replied quietly. "The swelling's going down in his leg, but they're worried about the skull fracture." She glanced quickly at Ginger and me. "But he'll be fine," she said with a slight smile.

"Any guess on how long he'll be in the hospital?"

Uncle Gus's eyes flashed at his wife. "Not long," he said quickly. He nodded in my direction. "Now, don't you worry these two children, Pauline."

We fell into silence and ate the stew and rolls. Outside the snow continued to fall.

As if God had set the world on daylight saving, the snow we had expected in November continued to fall through the last days of December. Daily, Uncle Gus drove Mom to the hospital while Ginger and I occupied ourselves by reading, playing games, and watching the few programs we were able to get on our television set. I had gotten into a regular, if not comfortable schedule. Each morning I retreated to the cellar and shoveled coal into the stoker. Then I removed the clinkers that had formed the previous day. Both washtubs were full to overflowing, but I wasn't strong enough to carry them up the steps. Finally, Uncle Gus struggled up the stairs with the washtubs and dumped them beside Dad's shed.

Following breakfast I shoveled the snow off the front steps before Uncle Gus showed up in his Hudson. But all of this order was going to quickly come to an end. Tonight was New Year's Eve, and then the day after tomorrow school would begin again. I had mixed emotions. In some respects school would be a welcome relief from the boredom of sitting around the house all day worrying about Dad, but it also meant I'd have to get up earlier to fill the stoker, then take a bath and get ready for school.

Since we lived nearly two miles from town, Uncle Gus and Aunt Pauline were the only neighbors we had. Consequently, none of my school friends lived close enough to visit them when it snowed. With school starting, I'd be able to share my life with someone other than Ginger.

We got into a routine. Every day Uncle Gus would drive Mom to the hospital to see Dad. Then, after they got back, all of us would eat supper at Aunt Pauline's. The report on Dad was discouraging; his condition hadn't changed.

One week after the accident, I had just finished shoveling the snow from the steps when Uncle Gus drove his Hudson into our driveway. I waved to him and went to tell Mom he had arrived. The tape on Mom's nose was fraying, and she had developed yellow, green, and purple bruises that gave her raccoon eyes. She was becoming more adept with her one good hand; however, she still needed help tying an apron.

"Rob, how would you like to come see your dad?" asked Mom. "Pauline's willing to have Ginger spend the day with her."

"Sure, Mom," I said, although I had some anxiety about spending all day in a hospital room.

We bundled Ginger up, and the three of us climbed into the car. Uncle Gus drove the quarter mile to his house and carried Ginger through the snow onto the porch. Aunt Pauline was waiting.

"Now, don't you worry. Ginger and I will have a grand day. We're going to make goodies so we can celebrate the new year." The two of them waved as Uncle Gus pulled back onto the road and we started to the hospital.

The road had been plowed but was still slippery in spots. Uncle Gus gripped the wheel tightly as he drove through our little town, past the church and the school, and on toward the hospital in Millville. The only sign of habitation was the fence that ran alongside the road. The fields lay unbroken, any ugliness covered with a pristine frosting of white.

There were only six rooms on Dad's floor of the

hospital. A nurses' station near the elevator guarded the hallway. As the elevator doors opened, a woman in a starched white uniform looked up from the pad she was writing on. She gave a barely perceptible nod. "Mrs. Henderson," she acknowledged.

"Any change?" asked Mom hopefully.

The nurse shook her head. "Dr. Mason was in earlier. He says the leg is beginning to heal and we can take it out of traction in the next couple of days." She shrugged her shoulders. "Other than that, no change." She smiled a thin smile at Uncle Gus. She ignored me.

We moved silently down the hallway to the end room. The door was closed, and Mom pushed it open tentatively. Dad was lying in bed, just as I had seen him a week before, but he looked thin and frail. His face was almost the whiteness of the bandage around his head. An inverted bottle hung on a pole by his bed and a tube snaked to a bandage on the back of Dad's hand. I watched the steady drip, drip, drip of fluid from the bottle. Another tube was attached to a bag filled with amber liquid and disappeared under the blanket on the bed. Mom sat down in the chair next to the bed and stroked Dad's hand.

"I'm back, John," she said evenly. "And I brought Rob."

Uncle Gus settled into a chair by the window and reached for a book that rested on the window sill. A folded Kleenex acted as a bookmark. There were no other chairs in the room. I knelt down next to Dad's bed.

"Talk to him, Rob. I'm sure he can hear what we're saying."

"Hi, Dad," I said haltingly. Mom nodded her head. "I sure hope you can come home soon. It's sure lonely without you." I reached out and patted his leg beneath the blanket. There was no response.

"Rob's been taking real good care of the house while I've been visiting you," Mom said as she stroked the back of Dad's hand. "And I don't know what we'd have done without Pauline and Gus."

Uncle Gus glanced up from his book at the sound of his name and smiled a thin little smile before returning to his reading. Nearly an hour passed while Mom spoke to Dad of how we were waiting to celebrate Christmas when he came home. Uncle Gus kept reading. My knees hurt from kneeling so long on the floor, and I stood up and went into the small bathroom to get a drink. Just as I came out of the bathroom, the door to Dad's room was pushed open and the nurse we had seen when we arrived marched into the room. I was afraid she'd make me leave. I remembered the two visitor rule.

She forced a thermometer into Dad's mouth and then said in her raspy voice, "If you'd step out into the hall for a few moments, please."

Mom rose slowly from her chair. Uncle Gus stuck the Kleenex back in his book and left it on the seat of his chair. The three of us walked out of the room and closed the door behind us. At the end of the short hall was a sofa upholstered in tan Naugahyde. Three of the upholstery buttons were dangling from threads, and the back of the sofa had a split revealing tufts of batting. The three of us sat down on it. I fiddled with one of the dangling buttons.

"I think he looks a little better, don't you?" Mom said hopefully.

Uncle Gus looked at the floor tiles and traced one with the toe of his boot. "You'd probably be better able to tell than me."

"He doesn't seem quite so pale," she continued. "And he seems to be breathing easier."

Uncle Gus nodded his head slowly. "I'm sure you're right, Elizabeth."

Mom twisted on her seat and looked out the window behind us. The snow had stopped falling, and the wind was blowing loose curls of flakes across the parking lot. "He will get better, you know. He'll be just fine."

We sat silently staring down the hall toward Dad's room. After an eternity the nurse backed out of his door, clipboard in hand, and returned to her station. "You can go back in," she said matter-of-factly.

"Thank you," said Mom as she launched herself to her feet and led the parade down the hall. There was no question about just two visitors.

The rest of the morning passed slowly. Uncle Gus continued to read his book, and Mom carried on her one-way conversation with Dad. After a while I wandered back into the hallway and to the tan sofa. A stack of magazines lay on a table next to it. I shuffled through them until I found an old copy of *Boys' Life*. I was just reading about how to carve a totem pole neckerchief slide when Uncle Gus walked out of Dad's room and came down the hall to where I sat.

"Hungry?" he asked. "It's half-past noon."

"A little," I admitted.

"Let's go get a hamburger. We'll bring something back for your mom."

He placed his hand on my shoulder as we rode down in the elevator. "Uncle Gus," I asked, "is Dad getting better?"

He squeezed my shoulder. "Your mom thinks so, and she has a powerful lot of faith," he replied.

"But what about you? You've been here every day. What do you think?"

The elevator doors opened, and we walked slowly through the foyer of the hospital. "Rob, my boy, I don't know. I really don't know. To be completely honest, I don't see the improvement your mother thinks she sees." He pushed open the hospital door. "I think it's going to be a long haul before your Dad's up to full speed, if you know what I mean." He patted my shoulder. "Now let's go get that hamburger."

The sun broke through the clouds briefly that afternoon as we began the drive back home, but by the time we arrived, the clouds had gathered and snow was falling again.

"Well?" asked Aunt Pauline, "How is he?"

"He's getting better," Mom said with a nod of her head.

Aunt Pauline looked over Mom's shoulder to Uncle Gus who barely, perceptibly shook his head from side to side.

"Ginger and I have been busy. We've made a whole refrigerator full of surprises for tonight. Isn't that right?"

Ginger nodded her head briskly. "We made cookies and a pie, and we got apple cider from the basement."

"It sounds great!" said Uncle Gus. "We'll all stay up until midnight, and we can welcome the new year."

After dinner we played Bingo while we listened to the radio. Guy Lombardo's orchestra was playing in New York. Since they were two hours ahead of us, we heard their celebration and joined in singing "Auld Lang Syne" as Aunt Pauline's grandfather clock was striking ten. Ginger was fighting hard to stay awake, but she finally gave up and curled into a ball on the couch. Aunt Pauline spread a blanket over her while Uncle Gus placed another couple of piñon pine logs in the fireplace. The pitch boiled out of the logs and spurted jets of flame as it dropped onto the coals. Mom stared, unblinking at the fire, her chin resting in her cupped hand, elbow on knee.

"It's going to be a great new year," said Aunt Pauline. "I can feel it in my bones." She went into the kitchen and returned with two pots and spoons. "You two young ones can bang on these," she said, handing me one of the pots. She placed the other one on the floor near the couch. "That is, if old sleepyhead wakes up."

The clock hand inched forward. Finally, the chime began to strike twelve. I began banging the pan and Ginger awoke to the noise. Aunt Pauline handed her the pot and spoon, and soon she joined in.

"Happy New Year!" cried out Aunt Pauline. She grabbed Uncle Gus and kissed him. "Happy New Year, Sweetheart," she said.

Mom kissed me on the cheek and Ginger on the top of her head. "Happy New Year, Sweet Pea," she said quietly.

Soon after that we bundled up in our coats, and Uncle Gus drove us home. The snow was swirling in the headlights and seemed to stream straight toward the windshield. We pulled into our driveway. Ginger and I climbed out of the backseat. Uncle Gus reached over and put his hand across Mom's shoulders. Quickly he leaned over and kissed Mom on the cheek. "Happy New Year, Elizabeth. I hope this next one is better than the last."

Mom pushed open the door to the car and then raised her hand to her face. "Happy New Year, Gus," she said as we hurried through the snow to the house.

❧ 10 ❧

Ginger and I slept late the next morning. By the time I began shoveling coal into the stoker, sunlight was streaming through a tiny hole in the cover over the coal chute. I could see the coal dust dancing in the beam. I wondered if Dad had ever noticed the sunbeam. A feeling of melancholy wrapped itself around me.

Last night's snow had stopped, and the first blue sky in a week hung overhead while I scraped the snow from the front steps. Mom came out and watched me, her old gray sweater pulled around her shoulders. She clutched it closed with her right hand. "Are you going to the hospital?" I asked.

She nodded her head. "In a few minutes. I've fixed

you some eggs and bacon." I could see her breath forming tiny clouds in the still morning air. She shivered, turned, and went into the house.

While I was eating breakfast there was a knock at the front door. When Mom answered it, Uncle Gus stood there on the front porch. I had not heard his car pull into the driveway. "Ready to go to the hospital, Elizabeth?"

"Let me say good-bye to the kids," she replied. Mom climbed the stairs to Ginger's room, and I heard faint mumbling as she talked to my sister. Uncle Gus waved at me from where he stood, just inside the front door.

"Mornin', Rob. Looks like it's going to be a beautiful day."

I nodded, my mouth full of eggs. He crossed the living room and leaned against the door frame. "School starts again tomorrow?"

"Yup," I said.

"Happy or sad about that?"

I shrugged my shoulders. "It's okay, I guess." I really was looking forward to school staring again, but I wasn't sure I wanted to admit it. I heard Mom's footsteps on the stairs.

She went to the hall closet before she looked into the kitchen. "I'll be back in a little while."

Uncle Gus reached for Mom's coat. "Let me help you with that, Elizabeth," he said. He took the coat and arranged it over Mom's shoulders.

"See you," he said to me as he led Mom out the front door.

I heard the toilet flush, and a moment later Ginger appeared in the kitchen. She sat down at the table and lifted a forkful of eggs to her mouth. "Yuck, they're cold," she said shaking her head from side to side.

"Well, they wouldn't be if you'd get out of bed," I said.

Ginger's lower lip stuck out. "Wasn't my fault we stayed up so late," she pouted.

I scraped the eggs and bacon off her plate back into the frying pan that was still on the stove and turned on the burner.

"I'll heat them up for you."

Ginger slipped off her chair and wandered into the living room. She returned with a Christmas present in hand. "Rob, the paper looks kinda funny," she said as she set the gift on the kitchen table.

I looked at the present. The paper was definitely fading.

"When do you think we're going to get to open them?" asked Ginger as she toyed with her food.

"When Dad comes home, I guess."

"How long's that going to be?"

"I don't know, Ginger. Mom's over at the hospital now." I tried to keep the annoyance from my voice but realized I had failed. A cold shiver ran down my spine.

Ginger continued to pick at her scrambled eggs. "I had a dream," she said quietly.

"So?"

She pushed the eggs into a pile on her plate. "Mom went to the hospital and Dad wasn't there. She looked all over for him. You and I were there, too. We looked all over the hospital, but Dad wasn't anywhere." She put down her fork and looked straight into my eyes. "Rob, do you think Dad's ever going to get better?"

"Sure," I said quickly. "Eat your eggs." For the second time that morning I felt my skin rise in goosebumps as a cold bolt shot though my insides. *What if Dad doesn't get better?* I thought. *What if he isn't here to take care of us and the orchard?* A feeling of near panic shook me. I looked out the window above the sink at the stark fingers of the trees pointing skyward. I knew that I could not, absolutely could not take care of a hundred acres of fruit trees. I did not have the physical strength, nor did I have the knowledge.

"Rob, are you all right?" asked my sister.

"I'm fine," I lied. "Hurry up and eat." I carried the

Christmas present back into the living room and put it under the tree. The needles of the spruce tree scratched the back of my hand. I could tell the tree was getting dry and looked almost as forlorn as the tattered presents lying on the floor beneath it.

"Ginger," I called to my sister, "when you've finished eating, we can take the decorations off the tree."

Dad had put the Christmas storage boxes in the basement. They were covered with a layer of coal dust. I blew the dust off, as best I could, and watched the beam of sunlight struggle through it before I carried the boxes upstairs.

We removed each ornament from the tree, wrapped it in tissue paper, and placed it in the thin cardboard boxes where they stayed year to year.

"Ow," said Ginger, "those needles are sharp." A spruce needle stuck out of the back of her finger. She pulled it out and stuck the finger in her mouth.

"I'll get the rest of them," I said.

"And I'll put them in the box," she replied.

Carefully the rest of the ornaments were removed from the tree. By standing on a chair I removed the ones from the top of the tree and then began taking off the strands of Christmas lights. By the time they were lying on the floor, I had scratches on the backs of both my hands. We plugged in the strands of lights, unscrewed the burned out bulbs and threw them away, then stuffed the cords into the tops of the boxes of ornaments.

The tree stood forlorn and bare, its dry limbs silhouetted in the sunlight streaming through the window.

"Rob, there's lots of needles on the floor."

I nodded my head. We moved the gifts onto the couch and swept up the dry, brittle needles, then put the gifts back under the drooping tree. The ribbons and paper were definitely showing the stress of repeated handling.

I retreated to my bedroom. The book I had threatened to read during our vacation lay taunting me on my dresser. I picked it up, lay down on my bed, and tried to get interested in it. I heard Ginger climbing the stairs.

"Rob," she called loudly from her room. "The drip's back."

The pot was half full of water. The drops of water from the ceiling had splashed a halo on the wooden floor around the pan. We wiped it up, replaced the pot with another, larger one, and emptied the first.

A wave of emotion swept over me. The dripping water was more evidence of things going wrong in our house and my inability to solve the problems. *Dad, you've got to get better*, I beseeched.

11

LATE IN THE AFTERNOON, Mom walked wearily through the front door. Clouds had begun to scud in from the northwest, and a brisk breeze swirled her coat as she closed the door behind her. "I'm home," she called.

I put a piece of paper in my book as a bookmark and stood up from the rocking chair in the front room. "How's Dad?"

"He's getting better," she said uncertainly. "There weren't many people at the hospital today. I thought there'd be more visitors. New Year's Day . . ."

I could tell she was struggling to control her voice. She shrugged her coat from her shoulders. "Let me help,"

I said. With her broken wrist, it was difficult for her to arrange her coat on a clothes hanger. I took the coat from her and hung it in the closet. She saw the naked spruce tree for the first time.

"Oh," she said as the back of her hand flew to her mouth.

"What's the matter, Mom?"

"Nothing." She turned her back to the tree, and I could see her eyes gleaming in the late afternoon sunlight as she fought back tears. "It's just . . . oh, I don't know." She nibbled on her knuckle. "It's silly."

"What, Mom?"

"I just thought we'd leave it decorated for your father."

"I'm sorry. We can put the decorations back on . . ." I looked at the scratches on the backs of my hands and remembered how sharp the needles were.

My mother turned back toward the tree. "No, no, it's all right. It's probably not safe. It's getting so dry." She sat down heavily on the couch.

Ginger raced down the stairs. "Mom, Mom, my ceiling's dripping again," she announced.

Mom's brow furrowed. "What?"

"The snow melted a little today, and the drip in

Ginger's room started. We put a bigger pot under it," I said.

Mom struggled to rise, then simply gave up and collapsed into the couch.

"Mom?" said Ginger, "What's wrong?"

Mom covered her face with her hands, and I could see her shoulders shaking as she leaned forward. Beams of sunlight from the setting sun fought their way through the gathering clouds and painted the cast on her arm a golden hue. I sat on the couch next to her and felt totally helpless. Ginger crouched at Mom's feet. In the silence I could hear the furnace grinding in the basement. And then Mom's shoulders stopped shaking and she straightened up. "We will not be beaten," she said resolutely.

"What?" whispered Ginger as she looked quizzically into Mom's face.

Mom's shoulders stiffened even more. "We can handle this."

I was unsure whether Mom meant the leaking roof or Dad's illness.

"We will not give up."

"Sure, Mom," I said, a little startled by the change in her demeanor.

"I think we will put the ornaments back on the tree,"

she continued. "Not the lights, after all we don't want to burn down the house, but the other ornaments, so they'll be there when your father comes home."

"Is he coming home soon?" asked Ginger.

"Yes, he is, Sweet Pea," said Mom, rising from the couch. "Very soon."

After dinner we hung the ornaments back on the tree.

❧ 12 ❧

VACATION WAS OVER, and the return to school was almost a relief. I awoke early to fill the stoker, bathe, and have breakfast before the school bus arrived. The ten days since the accident seemed to have stretched into a lifetime and, at the same time, seemed to have flown by as quickly as vacations often do.

The school bus pulled up in front of our driveway, and Mr. Fletcher opened the door. "Mornin', kiddos," he said. "Sorry to hear about your folks. How's your dad doing?"

"He's okay," I replied.

"Is he home, yet?"

I shook my head, "Pretty soon."

The bus door closed, and Ginger and I stumbled down the aisle to our seats as the bus lurched back onto the paved road. At each stop kids climbed on, wearing their new Christmas clothing. A few classmates waved as they took their seats, but all in all the bus was singularly quiet. I stared out the window as the bus continued its winding course to the school. When we arrived, Ginger scooted off toward her school, and I hung my coat in my locker and made my way to my first period English class.

The only person in the room when I entered was Steve Carlson. He was sitting at his desk reading. It was generally agreed that Steve was the smartest kid in the class. He was also the most obnoxious. He barely acknowledged my presence with a glance as I sat down two rows to the side of him. The clock in the front of the room showed that there was nearly ten minutes until class began. I considered going back onto the playground, but it seemed like too much trouble to go to my locker, get my coat, go outside for five minutes, and then reverse the process. I opened my English book and tried to remember where we'd left off before Christmas.

"Hey, Robert," said Steve. He called everyone by their full name.

"Yeah?"

"I heard your father fell off the roof."

I felt a cold hand clutch my stomach. "Yes, he did, Christmas Eve."

"What was he trying to do, catch Santa Claus?" he smirked.

I thought about trying to explain everything that had led up to the accident, but it seemed overwhelming. "Probably," I replied quietly.

"Want to see what I got for Christmas?" he asked.

I shrugged my shoulders. "I guess."

He reached into his pocket and pulled out a silver railroad pocket watch. He flipped open the cover and aimed the face in my direction.

Dutifully I slid over into the desk next to his and reached toward the watch. He pulled it back.

"Just look; don't touch," he said arrogantly.

"That's neat," I said, trying to keep the envy out of my voice.

"What did you get?" he queried.

"I don't know," I replied. "We're waiting for Dad to come home before we open our presents."

Steve barked out a laugh. "That's stupid," he said.

I felt rage welling up within me. I wanted to grab the watch from his hand and smash it. I started to rise from the desk when I heard Mom's voice in my head. *We can handle this.* I slid back over to my desk as Mrs. Hunter, our teacher, walked into the room.

"Good morning, gentlemen," she said. "I hope you had a pleasant holiday." Suddenly her face clouded. "Oh, Rob, I guess it wasn't very pleasant for you, was it?" At that moment the bell rang.

Before I could answer, a half dozen other kids burst through the door, each adorned with some evidence of the holidays. There was general commotion as, with the greed of youth, each tried to ascertain who had gotten the most for Christmas. Finally, the tardy bell rang, and Mrs. Hunter began to call the roll.

"I hope you all had a pleasant holiday," she said after marking the roll. Her eyes were fastened on mine. "And I'm sure you'd like to share it with me. So take out your notebooks. I'd like you to write three or four pages about your holiday experiences." A whispered groan bubbled through the class. "Please put your name and first period in the upper right-hand corner of the page." She turned and walked to the blackboard. Quickly, Mrs. Hunter drew a square that represented a piece of paper. She wrote "name" in the upper right-hand corner, with "1st period" beneath it. She then moved a few inches down the square and wrote "title" centered on the board.

"I'm going to give you most of the period to complete

this assignment. When you've finished, please tear the pages carefully from your notebook and fold the upper left-hand corner over." She returned to her desk and perched on the corner, facing the class. "Any questions?"

"Do you want it double spaced?" asked Mary Ann Perchon.

Mrs. Hunter shook her head, "No, single spaced will be fine." She looked up and down the rows. "Now if you need to check your spelling, you know where the dictionaries are. And I expect perfect grammar. Now, let's get to work."

She sat down at her desk and filled out the attendance sheet, then walked to the door and hung it on the spring clip screwed into the door frame. Then she began moving slowly up and down the rows, observing us work.

I opened the green cover of my notebook and began to write. There was some catharsis in writing about the events of Christmas Eve. It seemed as if in retelling the story, it lost some of its reality. But in the retelling I began to recognize the faith my mother had that my father would not only return home but recover fully. I wrote with a focused frenzy, filling the first page and moving quickly onto the second. I had grown out of the habit of telling my parents, especially my dad, that I loved them, but as I scribed my way through the bleakness of the night before Christmas, I felt a swelling within me of the love I had hidden under the guise of growing adolescent independence.

"You write very well, Rob," Mrs. Hunter said. I had not realized that she was reading over my hunched shoulders as I wrote. She patted me on the shoulder and moved silently up the row, pausing to read some of each Christmas essay. The hour passed quickly, and I was surprised when Mrs. Hunter announced there were only five minutes left to complete our writing and turn it in. I had written six pages, but as I read through them quickly, I was unsure whether I wanted to share my feelings with others.

I raised my hand. "Yes, Rob."

"Are you going to read these out loud to the class?"

She smiled gently. "No, I'll be the only one reading them."

Relieved, I tore the pages out carefully, folded the corner, and passed them forward. The bell rang, and we gathered our belongings and started toward the door.

"Rob," said Mrs. Hunter.

I turned back from the doorway. I was alone in the room with my teacher. "Yes?"

"There's no shame in expressing your love for your parents."

I could feel the color rising in my cheeks. I looked down at my shoes.

"Thank you for being brave enough to write what you really felt. Not many students are mature enough to do that."

Mrs. Hunter's second period class was beginning to arrive. "Thanks," I said and hurried into the hall.

The snow was falling heavily as we loaded back into the bus for the ride home. "How was school?" I asked Ginger.

"More fun that just sitting around the house doing nothing," she replied. "Miss Walquist says I can read well enough to move from the sparrows into the bluebirds," she smiled happily.

As Mr. Fletcher dropped off the Carlisle twins, the last to be let off before Ginger and me, the bus slid ominously on the shoulder of the road.

"I'm glad we don't have too much farther to go," he said tightly as he steered back onto the road. We traveled slowly down the pavement, with the bus throwing up rooster tails of slush and snow. At last he slid to a stop in front of our driveway.

"See ya in the morning," he said as Ginger and I climbed down the steps into the snow covering our driveway. The bus door closed behind us, and Mr. Fletcher maneuvered the bus back onto the road and disappeared around the bend toward Uncle Gus's house.

The odor of baking meat loaf drew me toward the kitchen as soon as we walked through the front door. Mom was struggling to spread a tablecloth on the table with one hand. "Let me do that," I said, taking the cloth from her.

"Thanks, Rob," she said cheerily. "How was school?"

"Okay," I replied.

"Homework?"

"Just math," I replied. "And I need to get the snow off the front steps."

"Well, you've got about an hour until supper."

"Do you need help?" I asked, indicating her cast.

"I'm getting pretty good, one-handed," she laughed. "Go ahead and do your homework."

Just then Ginger came into the kitchen. "How's my Sweet Pea?" Mom asked.

I climbed up the stairs and worked on my math. An hour later I closed my book and went downstairs to shovel the front steps. Ginger was sitting on a stool in the kitchen talking to Mom.

"Help me get some plates on the table and we'll eat."

The meat loaf steamed from its glass bread pan resting

on the top of the stove. The smell made my mouth water. Quickly we set the table and sat down to supper.

"I have some great news," Mom said. "The doctor says your father is stable."

I raised an eyebrow, "What does that mean?"

"It means they're going to show me how to take care of him, and then he can come home."

A smile exploded on Ginger's face, and I saw her shoot a glance through the doorway into the front room, where the Christmas tree stood, unlighted, but proud. After supper I walked past the tree and presents on my way to shovel the front steps. A thought, unbidden, entered my mind. Dad coming home is a better gift than anything that could be beneath the tree.

❁ 13 ❧

D AD DID NOT COME home the next day or the next, but on Saturday Mom announced proudly as Uncle Gus came to pick her up that they would be bringing him home today. Aunt Pauline came to stay with Ginger and me and help with the final preparations for Dad's homecoming. As if to celebrate this day, the snow had quit falling, and the world stood bright and clean in the winter sun.

I stood on the front porch and watched the Hudson pull out of the driveway. A line of icicles hung from the eaves of the house, reflecting the sun and creating a frosted fringe. Dad was coming home! All would be well. Tears threatened to spill from my eyes. The door opened, and Aunt Pauline stepped onto the porch. We stood together looking at the perfect whiteness of the world, the two of us nearly the same height. She reached over and put her hand on my shoulder.

"A great day, Rob. One we've all prayed for." Her voice was husky, and I could tell we shared feelings as well as size. "I hope your mother is up to taking care of your dad."

I nodded my head, "She will be. And we'll help."

"I'm sure you will," she said as she turned and walked across the porch, "and we will, too. I'm getting cold."

I stood a few more minutes on the porch and then went back into the house. Ginger was still sitting at the breakfast table. As I walked past the Christmas tree I noticed some of the needles had turned brown, and a fresh scattering of them lay on top of the sun-bleached packages beneath the tree.

"How long 'til Dad gets here?" she asked.

"Probably a couple of hours," answered Aunt Pauline. "Finish your breakfast, and then let's spruce up the house for his homecoming."

We occupied the next two hours dusting and vacuuming. Each of us glanced out the front window every chance we could, as if our looking would speed up Dad's arrival. The day dragged on as if in slow motion. We finally set up a Monopoly game on the kitchen table, and the three of us played a half-hearted game punctuated by glances out the window. Lunchtime came and went, and slivers of doubt began to stick in my soul. *What if something's gone wrong?* I thought. *What if something's happened to Dad?*

The pot in Ginger's room had begun to fill as the sun warmed the quilt of snow on the roof. After I emptied it and replaced it, I wandered out onto the front porch again and gazed down the roadway. Drops of water were forming on the tip of each icicle. *Tears of joy or sadness*, I wondered. And then the Hudson rounded the curve in the road and popped into view. My heart leapt within me. Quickly I went to the door and opened it.

"They're here!" I called out.

Uncle Gus pulled the Hudson far down our driveway. He helped Mom out of the car. I could see no one was in the backseat. My heart sank, and a cold chill ran down my spine. Then an ambulance pulled to a stop on the main road and began backing down our driveway behind the Hudson. I ran to Mom's side.

"He's home, Rob." Tears were flowing down her cheeks.

The attendants opened the back of the ambulance and lifted Dad out on a wheeled cart. It did not roll well through the snow, so they collapsed it and lifted the whole arrangement across the snow-covered lawn and up the front steps. Then they rolled the gurney through the front door. Mom led them down the hallway to their bedroom and peeled back the sheet and blanket. Dad was lifted easily into bed. I gazed at his face. His eyes were closed and his bristly cheeks sunken. It was as if a rag doll were lying on the bed.

A metal pole was positioned near the head of the bed, and the bottle of fluid attached to the tube running into the back of Dad's hand was suspended from it. I could also see a collection bag and a second tube that snaked out from under Dad's hospital gown. When the attendants had him positioned in the bed, Mom pulled the sheet and blanket up neatly over him.

Uncle Gus thanked the attendants and followed them out the door. In a moment we heard the ambulance pull away.

Dad's leg was still in a cast, but the bandages had been removed from his head. Stitches ran like a railroad track down the side of his head. Apparently they had shaved off his hair, and a mere quarter inch had regrown. His face was pale, but he appeared to be resting easily, although he looked thin and frail. My father had been a robust, take-charge individual before the accident, and

my eyes filled with tears as I looked at the helpless ver-
sion of him that lay in bed. Mixed emotions competed
within me. I was so glad to have him home, but while he
was in the hospital, there had been no constant and
visible reminder of his condition.

Mom fussed with the plastic line attached to his wrist.
The adhesive tape that crossed the back of his hand was
frayed and curling at the edge. Lovingly she lifted his
other hand with her good one and brought it to her lips.
"Welcome home, Sweetheart," she whispered. There
was no response.

Uncle Gus had returned to the doorway. He cleared
his throat, "I guess I'll be heading on home," he said
quietly.

"Thanks for everything, Gus," said Mom. "This has
been a terrible burden on you . . . spending every day
driving me back and forth to the hospital and all."

"No problem," he said. "Pauline and I are always here
to help." He lifted his hand in a partial salute. "Good to
have you home, John," he said, then turned and started
down the hallway toward the front room. "Pauline," he
called, "let's get out of here and let this family have a
reunion." And then, almost as an afterthought, "I put
the IV bottles in the kitchen."

Ginger had stood silently in the corner since Dad had been deposited in his bed.

"Mom, what happened to Dad's hair?" she asked.

"They had to shave it off."

"Why?"

"So they could take care of your dad's head." Gently she rubbed her hand on the stubble.

"Oh," said Ginger, not completely satisfied with the answer.

"Mom?"

"What? Sweet Pea."

"Are we going to open our presents, now?"

Mom continued to gently stroke Dad's head. After a moment, she said, "Let's wait until Dad can open them with us. Okay?"

"When will that be, Mom?"

Mom leaned over and kissed Dad softly. "Soon. Very soon."

❀ 14 ❀

DURING THE NEXT WEEK our routine changed, then stabilized. Mom had become quite proficient, even with her broken wrist. She could change the IV bottle and get it back on the stand without help. The county health nurse dropped in on Monday, Wednesday, and Friday afternoons to check on Dad. Although I usually saw her for only a few minutes after Ginger and I returned from school, she struck me as an unsmiling, no-nonsense person.

"He's getting better, don't you think?" asked Mom.

"Holding his own," was all the nurse replied as she inserted the IV needle into a new vein in Dad's hand. "These head injuries take time."

Mom nodded her head, "But I can see he's getting better," she replied firmly.

"If you say so," said the nurse as she secured the needle in place with a criss-cross of tape. She pulled her coat around her and repacked her black bag. "Sure wish this snow would stop." She marched to the front door. "I'll see you in a couple of days. Call if there's any problem."

"Thank you," said Mom as she turned back into Dad's bedroom.

The snow continued off and on through the rest of January. Dad's hair grew longer. The nurse had removed the stitches about a week after he came home, and the hair that was growing in along that curved line was snow white. We turned him frequently in his bed so that he wouldn't develop bedsores. He was unresisting, much like Ginger's Raggedy Ann doll. Except for infrequent moments when he exhaled a barely audible moan, there was no change that I could see. He lay with his eyes closed, but Mom insisted that he was getting better. Often when I arrived home from school she would be sitting beside his bed, holding his hand, and talking to him of events that had happened earlier in their lives. I could see no response from Dad.

More of the needles on the Christmas tree turned brown and dropped in forlorn piles on top of the sun-bleached gifts. We had grown so used to the tree that neither Ginger nor I paid much attention to it standing there in the front room. We were careful not to brush against it since the result was a cascade of needles and often a few sharp jabs in the hand or arm. Ginger had stopped asking when we were going to open our gifts.

Either Uncle Gus or Aunt Pauline or both dropped in nearly every day.

"You ought to let me get rid of that tree," Uncle Gus said one evening. "It's a fire hazard."

Aunt Pauline had been there all afternoon cooking supper for us. The aroma of her apple crisp filled the air.

"Thank you, Gus, but we're keeping it to celebrate Christmas with John."

Uncle Gus snorted softly and shook his head. Aunt Pauline swatted him with the wooden spoon in her hand.

An enormous snowstorm welcomed February. Snowplows tried vainly to keep ahead of the blizzard, but the school bus was barely able to navigate the road to our house. One afternoon Ginger and I fought our way through a foot of snow to the front steps. Apparently Uncle Gus had been there and cleared them of snow. The phone rang as we stepped through the door.

"Hello?" I said, picking up the receiver.

"Is your mother there?" I recognized the voice of Miss Steenblick, the nurse.

"Just a minute." I covered the mouthpiece with my hand and called down the hallway, "Mom, phone for you."

"Hold on."

I noticed the puddle of melted snow forming around my feet and placed the phone on the counter before squeaking across the kitchen to the back door, where I pulled off my boots. I grabbed a dish towel from where it stuck through a cupboard door handle and wiped up the water. Mom frowned at me as she entered the kitchen and picked up the phone.

"Hello?" She paused for nearly a minute. "I see. Tomorrow?" she said hopefully. There was another long pause. "We're fine. I'll see you when you can get here. Good-bye." She hung up the phone. Her shoulders sagged for a few seconds; then she straightened them. "Miss Steenblick can't make it through the snow," she said to me.

"How's Dad?" I asked in part of the ritual that surrounded our arriving home each afternoon.

"Getting better," Mom replied, completing the ritual.

Ginger ran down from her room and joined us as we

made the pilgrimage to Dad's bedside. Mom took her usual place on the chair next to the bed. I noticed that the cast on her wrist had frayed and softened where her fingers emerged. She kept a knitting needle on the nightstand and often stuck it down inside the cast to scratch an almost unceasing itch as her wrist healed.

Dad's hair was well over an inch long now and stuck out, making his head look like a dark brown cocklebur. The track of white ran from above his right ear around the back of his head. He was in need of a shave. Since it was Monday, Miss Steenblick had not been to our house since Friday. She had tried to teach Mom how to shave Dad's face, but due to her broken wrist, Mom had been unable to pull the slack skin on his face taut. With a snort and a shrug, the nurse just made the shave part of her visit and routine.

Dad's condition had changed. But it had changed so slowly in the month that he had been home that I had not noticed it. It was much, I suppose, as when I realized I could reach the top of the refrigerator for the first time. I could not remember any specific day in which I had grown taller; it had just happened. But now, standing at the foot of Dad's bed, I became acutely aware of how frail he looked.

Before the accident Dad had been a tall, robust man

who could do anything that needed to be done around our house. Here he lay, almost skeletal. A memory flitted through my head like a butterfly. I remembered my Grandfather Henderson's funeral. I was barely five years old when he died and had not wanted to go to the funeral. I had never seen a dead body before, and I was frightened; but Mom had insisted.

When we reached the mortuary, I threw a tantrum in the backseat of the car but to no avail. I was dragged inside. Most vivid in my memory was the smell of flowers that assaulted us as we walked slowly down the wine-colored carpet. The open coffin was lighted with a floor lamp at each end, the light thrown upward toward the ceiling. Floral sprays were arranged around the coffin. Dad picked me up and walked to where a waxen replica of my grandfather lay.

"They've done a good job," Dad whispered.

Mom nodded her head and said nothing. She was wearing a black dress and a black pill box hat with a veil that she kept lifting so she could dab her eyes with a tissue.

My grandfather had been a simple man. I had never seen him dressed in anything but flannel shirts and overalls. The mannequin in the coffin was dressed in a navy blue suit with a white shirt and blue tie. Mom leaned over and kissed Grandpa on his forehead. I reached out my hand and touched the back of his hand. It was cold and stiff. My hand recoiled from the touch.

And now as I stood at the foot of the bed looking at my father's face, I saw the same slackness, the same waxiness I had seen in my grandfather's face as he lay in his coffin.

15

UNCLE GUS KNOCKED on the front door, then let himself in. "Hello," he called, "anyone home?"

"Hi," I waved from the couch.

"Oh, Rob, I didn't see you," he started. "Is your mom ready for the big day?"

"I'm sure she is," I said. "I'll get her."

"No need," my mother said as she entered the front room from the hallway. "I'm ready." Uncle Gus helped her arrange her coat around her shoulders.

"Well, Elizabeth, at least you'll be able to put your coat on proper for the trip home."

"I'm looking forward to it," she smiled. "Rob, I've

changed your Dad's IV bottle. You know the number to call if there's any problem."

I nodded my head.

"Thanks, Sweetheart," she said.

Then the two of them walked out the front door. "I'll be so glad to get this cast off," I heard her say to Uncle Gus as the door closed.

After finishing the chapter of my book, I walked down the hall to check on Dad. Since it was Saturday, Miss Steenblick had been there the previous afternoon to check on him and shave off his stubble. When Mom gets home, she'll be able to do that, I thought. For some reason that thought filled me with both joy and apprehension. I was happy that Mom's wrist had healed and the itching torment of the last month would be ended, but it also meant that we were becoming less dependent on Miss Steenblick, and for some reason that thought chilled me to the bone. My mind flitted into the future, and I saw Mom and me still taking care of an old man who lay in my father's bed.

Selfishness and guilt fought within me. I knew I should be happy to be able to take care of Dad, but a lifetime of being shackled to his helpless frame seemed unbearable. And then an unbidden upsurge of love for my father overcame me. I knelt by his bed and held his hand in mine. "Dad, I'm sorry," I said softly. Bright sunlight streamed into his room. I let go of his hand and crossed the room to the window. The orchard lay untouched, and the snow was melting quickly in the early March sunshine.

"Whatchadoin'?" asked Ginger from the doorway. She rubbed the sleep from her eyes with the back of her fists.

"Just checking on Dad," I replied. "Mom's gone to get the cast taken off her arm. Want some breakfast?"

She nodded her head and shuffled down the hallway.

"We can handle this," I whispered to my father as I followed Ginger to the kitchen.

Two hours later I heard a car pull into the driveway. Uncle Gus opened the door of the Hudson, and my mother emerged with both arms in the sleeves of her coat. Uncle Gus took her by the elbow and helped her up the stairs. Ginger and I pulled the door open.

"Look," said Mom, "no cast." Uncle Gus helped her remove her coat. "Thank you, Gus, I think I can hang it up myself." She opened the closet door and removed a hanger.

I looked at her left arm. With all the hours spent in the orchard, my mother had a perpetual tan, which faded some during the winter months but was still noticeable. The arm that had been ensconced in plaster was nearly as white as the cast had been, and a few shards of dead skin still remained. She rubbed her forearm and wrist briskly, and a cloud of powdery skin erupted into the beams of sunlight streaming into the room.

"How does it feel, Elizabeth?" asked Uncle Gus.

"Weak," said Mom with a smile, "and a little stiff. But it will be fine." She flexed her fingers. "It feels so good to have the cast off." Her arm had grown almost as thin as Dad's. She turned it in the sunlight. "Looks like it needs a little exercise, though," she laughed.

"Well, I guess I'll be going," said Uncle Gus. He looked at the remnants of our Christmas tree. The few needles that remained on the tree were all russet brown. Most had fallen in indistinct piles on the floor and the presents.

"Why don't you let me take that out for you?" he said, pointing toward what was left of the tree.

Mom shook her head. "We're still waiting to celebrate Christmas." Mom glanced toward the hallway. "With John."

Uncle Gus nodded and turned toward the door. "Have you thought about pruning, Elizabeth?"

"What?"

"Another couple of weeks, and it will be time to prune the peaches. You've got about five hundred trees that need attention. Have you thought about who is going to prune them?"

Mom's shoulders slumped. "I don't know, Gus, maybe they won't get pruned this year."

Uncle Gus snorted, "You can't leave them or it'll take years to give 'em the proper shape. They've got to be pruned. You've got to get sunlight down into the middle of the tree to get a proper crop."

"We'll do it," I said quietly, remembering my promise to Dad.

Uncle Gus snorted again, "You have any idea how long it will take to prune five hundred trees, boy?"

"Not really," I shook my head.

"If you started today, there'd be peaches ready to harvest before you got done."

"But Dad's always done it himself," I countered.

"Your Dad knew what he was doing, and he worked sunup 'til it was too dark to do justice," he replied.

"We'll do it, Gus," said Mom quietly as she straightened her shoulders. "Rob and I."

"And who'll take care of John while you're out in the orchard?"

Mom turned toward Uncle Gus. "I don't know how it will all work out, but it will." She smiled a thin little smile. "Thank you for taking me to the hospital. You and

Pauline have been a godsend." She turned and started down the hallway toward Dad's room.

Shaking his head, Uncle Gus pulled open the door and left. I looked out the window toward the expanse of peach trees. They stood as silent sentinels, arms raised. Next Saturday, I thought, we'll start pruning.

"Rob," Mom called from Dad's bedroom. "Come help me turn your father. My wrist is still too weak to do it myself."

After we finished the now familiar routine of rolling Dad onto his side and propping him up with pillows, I turned to my mother. "I'll start pruning the trees next Saturday."

She patted my shoulder, "That will be good, Rob." She stared out the window toward the orchard, "But Gus is right. We'll never finish it ourselves."

"We can handle it," I replied.

❧ 16 ❧

SATURDAY MORNING arrived. The air was crisp and frosty as I entered the shed behind our house and found Dad's pruning shears. I could see my breath forming clouds as I exhaled. The north side of each tree in the orchard still had a small drift of snow lying in the shadow of its trunk. The ground was soft and felt spongy beneath my feet as I walked to the far border of our orchard. Mud stuck to the bottoms of my boots, adding weight with every step. Even though I was wearing my jacket, I shivered a bit in the early morning air.

I had not been out this far into the orchard since before Christmas. The snow had been heavy and deep. I remembered Dad's concern about the deer nibbling the branches of the trees but had no idea what I could have done to prevent it, had I discovered that to be the case. Finally I reached the fence line that marked the end of our property and marched resolutely toward the southeast corner, where the peach trees began. Someone had tied strips of red and yellow cloth to the branches of several of the trees. I wondered if Dad had done that in an attempt to frighten the deer. It was evident from the piles of raisin-shaped droppings that the effort had not been entirely successful. I could see where many of the trees had been browsed.

I was so intent inspecting the damage to the trees that an irregular clicking sound barely registered in my brain, but when it did I realized I was not alone in the orchard. Uncle Gus was a dozen trees away from me, snipping away with his pruning shears. It was obvious from the pile of clippings on the ground that he had already finished pruning fifteen or sixteen trees. He apparently had been watching my approach.

"Morning, Rob," he said as he continued snipping. His bony frame was dressed in a red-and-black plaid shirt and overalls. The flaps of his cap were pulled down over his ears, and he was wearing a pair of leather gloves. "Thought we'd better get an early start."

"Good morning," I stammered.

Snip, snip, snip. "Ever pruned a peach tree?"

I shook my head. "I've watched Dad, though."

Uncle Gus paused in his snipping. "Well, let me show you how it's done," he said, walking toward the tree where I stood. "The idea is that we're trying to form a bowl shape," he said. "But if the bowl gets too wide, the branches can't bear the weight of the fruit. Okay?"

I nodded my head, still unsure what I was to do.

"Then we need to cut out these suckers in the middle." He quickly snipped a dozen new growth branches that angled up in the center of the tree. "We've got to let the sunlight get into the middle of the bowl." He continued snipping. "Then we've got to keep the whole tree at a manageable size." Snip, snip. "Notice that the buds are on the new growth. Of course if they were cherries, they'd be on last year's growth," he said, pointing with the tip of his shears to a fur-covered bud. "If a branch is too small to support a peach, we need to clip it off." Snip, snip. "A bad haircut will grow back, but bad pruning can ruin a tree, so be careful."

It was clear Uncle Gus knew what he was doing and equally obvious that I had no idea how to prune a tree.

"Now," said Gus, slipping the retaining clip over his shears and dropping them into the back pocket of his overalls, "you try it, and I'll supervise."

I nodded my head and bravely inspected the tree next to the one that Uncle Gus had shaped to perfection. I unclipped my pruning shears and selected a branch. Uncle Gus shook his head and pointed to one next to it. I felt my cheeks flare. I had no idea why the branch I'd chosen was the wrong branch. I snipped off the one Uncle Gus had indicated. Thirty minutes later, with much coaching, I'd finished pruning the tree. The beginning of a blister was forming on my hand where I'd squeezed the handles of the pruning shears. I realized quickly why I should have worn my gloves. I looked back toward the house from our hillside perch and wondered about trudging through the soft soil of the orchard the half mile back to the house to get them. I could see the snow had melted from the roof, and a fleeting question about the leak in Ginger's room raced through my mind.

"Rob, I have an idea. Why don't you let me prune the trees, and you gather the clippings and pile them out in the field so we can burn them?"

A wave of indignation swept over me. "You don't think I can prune a tree right, do you?"

Uncle Gus sighed loudly, "Do what you want to do, boy," he said, "but somebody's got to clean up all that tangle or we can't run the tractor down these rows to keep the weeds down." He unclipped his shears and began silently working the next tree. As he finished with it I heard a call from over the fence toward Uncle Gus's house. A dozen or more men were making their way through Uncle Gus's orchard toward the fence line that separated our properties. Uncle Gus raised his arm and waved. "Over here," he called loudly.

I recognized all the men and even knew the names of two or three of them. Uncle Gus spread the strands of wire on the fence by standing on the lower one and holding the upper wire as high as he could stretch it. The men stooped and slid through the fence.

"Morning, Gus," said one of the men, whose name I could not recall. He touched his hand to the bill of his baseball cap in an informal salute. There was a chorus of greetings that rumbled through the group. "Looks like the deer have been here," one of the men said, fingering the frayed end of a peach twig, "but it don't look too bad."

"This here's John's boy, Rob," Uncle Gus said, pointing his shears in my direction. "He's going to haul the clippings back into the field, aren't you, boy?" he continued, waving his hand toward the empty field beyond the orchard. "Thanks for your help."

"Happy to do it," replied the nameless man. "You know what they say, 'Many hands make light work.'"

The volunteers moved quickly into the peach trees, and within seconds a tangle of branches began to grow beneath a dozen trees. I scurried amongst the men, picking up the clippings and carrying them to a growing pile in the field. The sun continued its upward climb as the platoon of pruners marched slowly through the peach trees, the chorus of clicking almost melodious as the tangle of clippings grew. I scampered as quickly as I could up and down the rows, unsuccessfully trying to keep up with the men.

Other than the sound of the shears, it was a silent army that snipped and shaped the bowls of the trees. My back ached, and by the time the sun was directly overhead, I had scraped and scratched my hands until they were raw. But well over half the peach trees had been pruned.

"Yoo-hoo, Gus!" I looked toward the fence line and saw Aunt Pauline waving her hand. She was wearing overalls and her wool-lined coat and was dangling a large basket from her other hand. "Lunch is ready," she called.

"Let's take a break," Uncle Gus said, pulling off his hat and wiping his brow. Sometime during the day he had tied the earflaps back over the top of the cap. "Pauline's fixed some sandwiches." The crew of pruners gathered at the fence line. I hung back, unsure of whether I was included. "You, too, Rob," said Uncle Gus, thrusting his chin in my direction. "Come on over and get something to eat."

The basketful of liverwurst, ham and cheese, and peanut butter sandwiches was consumed in a few minutes. Aunt Pauline had also brought a gallon jug of coffee and some paper cups. "You'll have to drink it fast, before it melts the wax on the cups," she said as she poured the steaming liquid.

The men thanked Aunt Pauline and turned back to the task at hand. "If we keep up this pace, we should be done before four o'clock," said a short, heavyset man with a three-day growth of salt-and-pepper beard. I returned to carrying armfuls of branches to the field and throwing them on the growing pile.

Before the sun set in the west, the last of the peaches had been pruned. Each of the men walked down the row he had pruned and picked up the remaining branches and twigs that lay on the ground. By the time they had thrown the branches onto the pile, it had grown to thirty feet across and was higher than a man.

"We'll let them dry for a few weeks; then we'll have us a bonfire," said Uncle Gus. "I sure do appreciate the help," he continued, pulling off his glove and shaking hands with each of the men, who climbed back through the fence and waved good-bye as they crossed Gus's orchard to their cars and trucks.

I had mixed feelings of gratitude and depression. I felt, somehow, as if I had failed my father by not completing the task myself but, deep in my heart, I knew that without the help we had received, the task would never have been completed. Uncle Gus put his hand on my shoulder.

"A good day's work, Rob," he said as he gazed over the peach trees and then back at the pile of branches.

"I . . . we . . . sure appreciate the help," I stammered.

"That's what neighbors and friends are for," he said, pulling the earflaps on his cap down over his ears. "Sure is a cold wind," he complained as he folded himself through the fence and walked stiffly toward his house.

❧ 17 ❧

I RETURNED THE PRUNING shears to the tool shed, then before going into the house, scraped the mud from the soles of my boots on the edge of the back porch steps. I could smell a ham simmering in the oven, but the kitchen was dark. I turned on the light and searched in the medicine cabinet near the sink for hand lotion. My hands were oozing blood from a number of the deeper scratches, and the blisters had popped. I washed my hands in the sink and dried them on a dish towel that was looped through the handle of the silverware drawer. My hands were stiff from the cold and were beginning to swell. I slathered on the lotion, turning my nose up at the floral scent and wincing at the sting.

The Christmas tree still stood in the living room, now scarcely more than a bare stick with a few crisp brown needles clinging tenuously to the twigs at the end of the branches. Mom vacuumed the pile of needles under the tree every morning, but there were fewer left to drop each day. The shiny ornaments hung in bizarre contrast to the bare branches. The tops of the brightly wrapped presents had sun-bleached to an almost uniform color-lessness, and the Scotch tape that held the wrapping together had begun to look like shiny strips of water with bubbles trapped beneath the surface. The once colorful wrapping paper was as dry and brittle as the remaining needles on the tree.

I had put too much lotion on my hands and ended up wiping part of it on the legs of my pants as I made my way down the hall to Dad's room. Mom was sitting in her usual spot at the head of the bed, barely visible in the waning sunlight. Her hands were folded in her lap. "Oh, Lord," she was whispering as I reached the doorway, "this is a good man. Such a good man. Help him, Lord, to regain his strength." She paused, and I could see sparks of sunlight through the tears coursing down her cheeks. "But if that is not to be, please give me the strength to accept thy will."

I felt as if I were an intruder in a very private moment. I turned as quietly as I could, trying not to disturb Mom.

"Rob, is that you?" she said huskily.

"Sorry, Mom," I replied as I cleared my throat.

"How did your day go?" she said as she wiped at her cheeks with her hands.

"Okay, I guess."

"How do the peach trees look?" she asked.

"They're all pruned," I replied.

She rose from her chair, "But how? I mean, I'm sure you . . . you know. There are just too many trees for one . . . one man." She spread her hands and hunched her shoulders.

"Uncle Gus and a bunch of his friends helped," I said, neglecting to mention that I had pruned only one tree.

Her hands flew to her mouth. "Oh, Rob, how can we ever repay him?" Tears overflowed her eyes again.

"I dunno," I said shrugging my shoulders. "How's Dad?"

My mother looked down at my father's frail frame. She looked lovingly at him for a moment, and then her shoulders straightened and she looked at me. "He's getting better. Much better."

I stood in the doorway trying to rub the last vestiges of lotion into my hands as I saw my mother lean and kiss my father gently on his lips. Then she stood and said, "I think it's time we had supper."

I followed her down the hallway. At the bottom of the steps she called, "Ginger, time for supper."

I could hear my sister scrambling around in her room. "Coming," she replied, as she bounded down the stairs. A few remaining needles on the tree trembled and dropped onto the gifts below.

"What's wrong with your hands?" asked Mom as we sat at the table.

"Nothing," I said as I tried to grip a fork with my swollen fingers.

"Let me see," she said and reached across the table and turned my hand palm upward. My fingers had swollen like sausages, and the palm of my hand was criss-crossed with scratches. The popped blisters looked like white bubbles against the redness of my palms. I looked at my mother's face as she inspected my hand. I could see the threat that tears would flow again.

"I'm fine, Mom." I flexed my fingers slowly. "Just a few scratches from pruning." I was saved from further inter-rogation by the telephone.

Mom picked up the receiver, "Hello?" She covered the mouthpiece with her hand and whispered to me,

"Can you slice the ham, Rob?" She stepped partway into the hall.

I nodded and tried to grasp the knife securely enough to cut slices of ham. I finally succeeded in cutting a piece for Ginger and lifting it onto her plate. The handle of the knife seemed to burn into my hand. With some difficulty I finished cutting a slice for Mom and me.

"I don't know how we can thank you enough," my mother said into the phone. "Yes, it's still leaking, but I can't ask you to . . ." Her voice trailed off as she listened for several seconds. "If you're sure." She grew silent. I could see tears welling up again. "Thank you. Goodbye."

She hung up the phone and leaned against the doorjamb for a minute, her eyes closed, her mouth pursed, and her chin trembling. She pulled a wad of Kleenex from the pocket of her housedress, wiped her cheeks, and blew her nose.

"That was Gus," she said quietly as she returned to the table. "He's going to come over Monday morning and try to fix the leak in the roof." She shook her head. "I don't know how we'll ever repay his kindness." Sitting down, she only toyed with the ham and potatoes on her plate.

I looked at my mother's face and could see how difficult it was for her to have to rely on others to get things done. I knew how she felt. I pictured the pile of peach limbs waiting to be burned, remembering the shame I had felt in not being able to take care of the orchard. At that moment I vowed that if anyone was ever in need, and I had the skill or knowledge necessary, I would help.

Awkardly I picked up my fork and ate my supper, wincing as I continued to find new spots of pain. After we finished eating, I attempted to help Ginger clear the table, but my fingers refused to flex well enough to grasp the plates.

"Let me see those hands," Mom said softly. I held them out, palms up in front of her. She drew a breath. "Oh, Rob," she shook her head slightly, "why didn't you wear gloves?"

I shrugged my shoulders.

"Go wash them," she said, holding my hands tenderly. "You've got dirt in some of the scratches." She shooed me toward the bathroom.

When I returned to the kitchen she had the brown iodine bottle in her hand. Instructing me to hold out my hands, she dipped the little glass wand on the cap into the iodine and painted the scratches until both hands were nearly covered with the orange-brown liquid. When she finished with the iodine, she screwed the cap on tightly and then rubbed bag balm into my hands. I gritted my teeth to keep from crying out from the pain.

Mom's eyes were glistening as she finished. "Thank you, Rob, for taking care of the orchard."

"I didn't do much," I replied honestly.

She took my hands in hers. "You did all that you could do," she replied, "and that's all anyone can ask."

❀ 18 ❀

Sunday morning I awoke in agony. My fingers simply refused to bend, and my puffy hands felt as if they were on fire. I rolled out of bed and made my way to the bathroom. With difficulty I managed to fill the sink with cold water and immerse my hands. The burning sensation went away and was replaced with a dull ache from the cold water. I pulled my hands out of the water and tried unsuccessfully to flex my fingers. I patted my hands on the towel hanging next to the sink and began to feel the burning sensation returning. I plunged my hands back into the sink.

Ginger appeared at the bathroom door, carrying the

pot of water from her room. "What's the matter, Rob?" she asked.

"Nothing," I said, gritting my teeth.

She dumped the water into the toilet and went back to her room to place it under the drip from her ceiling.

I had been unable to manipulate the buttons on my shirt or jeans the previous night and had slept in my clothes. I had managed to kick my boots off, thankful that they did not have laces. Ginger reappeared at the bathroom door.

"I need to use the bathroom, Rob," she said urgently.

I pulled my hands out of the sink and dabbed them dry on the towel. The burning sensation was not as severe as it had been.

"Hurry, Rob!"

Mom was fixing breakfast, and the heady aroma of biscuits and gravy drew me downstairs to the kitchen.

"Morning, Rob," my mother said cheerfully. "How are your hands?"

"Better," I lied.

"Let me see," she said, giving the gravy a vigorous stir before setting the spoon down in the little ceramic holder I had made in the third grade. She took my hands in hers and examined them. "They look sore," she said.

"They hurt a little bit," I admitted.

"Flex your fingers," she gently commanded.

I tried to bend my fingers, but they refused to obey. And the burning sensation began to grow as I struggled. "I guess they're still kind of stiff," I said.

"Oh, Rob," my mother said. She turned her head away from me to hide the tears. "I wish I knew why we've been asked to pay this terrible price."

"It's not so bad," I replied, still trying to flex my fingers.

Mom shook her head slowly. We heard Ginger's footsteps as she came down the stairs. "I'm hungry," she said as she wandered into the kitchen.

"Pull up your chair, Sweet Pea. It'll be ready in a minute."

Mom gave the gravy a final stir and removed the biscuits from the oven. Deftly she popped a couple of them onto each of our waiting plates and then spooned the sausage-laden gravy over them, making my mouth water.

"Can you manage your fork?"

"Sure," I replied. But I could not. My fingers absolutely refused to bend enough to hold my fork. Ginger stifled a laugh behind her hand as I vainly tried to pick up the utensil.

"Don't laugh," Mom said sternly. "Rob sacrificed himself for our well-being."

Ginger continued to giggle. "He's got fat fingers," she said, pointing at my unsuccessful attempt to pick up the fork.

"That's enough!"

Ginger quit laughing. Mom picked up my fork, cut a piece of biscuit and placed it in my mouth. My face flared at being fed like a baby, but the food tasted wonderful. It was almost worth the wounded pride.

The rest of the day passed in painful slowness. I could not successfully hold a book in my hands and turn the pages. Periodically my hands began to throb, and it felt as if my fingers had swollen to the point that if I tried to move them, the skin would split. Mom wrapped some ice cubes in a kitchen towel and pounded them with a hammer until they were reduced to snow. She laid the towel across my upturned palms and loosely tied the ends together. My hands ached with a dull pain until they finally went numb. Ginger turned on our yellow-screened Hoffman and vainly tried to find a program that interested her.

When at last the sun set, I climbed the stairs to my bedroom after having faced the ignominy of having my mother unbutton my shirt for me. At least my hips were slim enough that I was able to jamb my thumbs into the waistband and wiggle out of my buttoned jeans. With difficulty I shed my shirt and climbed in between the sheets of my bed. It was difficult to find a comfortable position, but at last I dropped into a fitful sleep.

I awoke the next morning to the sound of Mom's tread on the stairs. Sunlight was streaming through the windows of my room. My hands were somewhat better, but still painful to move. My mother opened my door slowly.

"Morning, Rob. How are your hands?"

"Getting better." I flexed them as much as they'd flex. "What time is it?" I said with some alarm.

"Ginger's already left for school. I think you'd better stay home today and get your hands better."

A minor conflict erupted in my breast. It seemed as if I should be protesting the need to stay home, and yet I was delighted with a previously unscheduled vacation day. I hung my head, "If you say so, Mom." And as I hung my head I smiled.

"Why don't you climb into the bathtub?" she said as she walked out of my room. "I've filled it for you."

I eased myself into the steaming tub and immersed my swollen hands. As they sank beneath the water, sharp pains shot though both hands, and I clenched my jaw to keep from screaming. After a few moments the pain subsided and I sank back into the water. A few blissful moments later I heard a noise above me on the roof. Alarmed, I sat up in the tub, then remembered that Uncle Gus was going to try to patch the roof. Somewhat guiltily I settled back under the water.

Eventually the water cooled, and I pulled the plug out by wrapping the tethering chain around my big toe. But I continued to lie in the tub as the water gurgled down the drain, forming a whirlpool as it went. The noise on the roof continued.

I found that some flexibility had returned to my fingers, and I was able to pull a towel off the rack and dry myself. My mother had left a clean pair of underwear on the toilet seat, and I pulled them on. Then I hurried down the hall to my room and dressed myself in jeans and a T-shirt. I had succeeded in pulling my socks off the night before with my toes, but found I could not easily pull clean ones back on my feet. So barefooted, I padded down the stairs to the kitchen. Mom had left breakfast for me and had apparently gone outside to help Uncle Gus.

With some difficulty I ate my bowl of oatmeal and a piece of toast. Then I slid my chair back under the table and was reaching for a glass of milk when I heard the front door open.

"Well, I think we've taken care of the leak,

Elizabeth," I heard Uncle Gus say. I could hear him stamping his feet on the front porch.

"Gus, I just don't know how we can ever thank you," replied my mother.

"Just trying to be neighborly," he said. I heard the front door close.

"You and Pauline have done so much," continued my mother. "First you drove me to the hospital every day, then you pruned the orchard, and now you've fixed the leak in the roof. I can't believe how willing you've been to help."

Uncle Gus cleared his throat. He spoke more softly. "Elizabeth, I hope you know there's nothing I wouldn't do for you," he said. "I know how hard this has been on you, John being heaved up, I mean. And I just want you to know that if you have . . ." He paused for a moment before continuing, "have . . . other needs, physical needs, I'd be glad to take care of those, too."

I heard my mother's quiet gasp. "What do you mean, Gus?" She said it so softly I could barely understand her words.

Uncle Gus cleared his throat again, "Well, you're a young, healthy woman, Elizabeth, and I'm sure there are needs and desires you have that John hasn't been able to fulfill. I'm offering to take care of you in those ways," he said.

I felt the slap almost as much as I heard it. Mom's voice took on a steely tone I had never heard. "Gus, leave now, and never set foot in this house again."

"Elizabeth," he moaned, "I didn't mean no harm. I—"

"Out!" she commanded. At that moment I knocked the butter knife into the sink. It clattered loudly.

"Who's there?" Gus cried out in alarm.

I stretched to my full height and walked around the corner into the living room. "I am," I said, with as much force as I could muster.

"I believe you were going," my mother said as she wrenched the door open.

Uncle Gus gathered as much dignity as he could under the circumstance and marched out the door. Mom slammed it shut behind him before she dissolved into tears.

❀ 19 ❀

THE YELLOW LIGHT from our Hoffman television flickered across the front room. The only other light came from a single floor lamp in the corner. The pitiful skeleton of our Christmas tree stood in mute silence. The ornaments reflected the flickering images of *Your Show of Shows* as Sid Caesar and Imogene Coca performed another of their insane skits. Ginger and I laughed. Mom sat hollow-eyed in the rocking chair.

I pushed myself up from the couch and approached her. "Mom, what's wrong?"

She shook her head almost imperceptibly, "Nothing, Rob," she whispered.

"It's time to turn Dad," I said, reaching for her hand.

She took my hand, I pulled her to her feet, and we walked down the hall to Dad's room.

The light from his bedside lamp accentuated the deep hollows of his cheeks. He had been home now nearly three months, and I could see no change in him. He still lay, unresisting in his bed, tethered to his plastic life-lines. Miss Steenblick, his nurse, continued her visits three times a week. Occasionally, Dr. MacArthur came by. He would check Dad's lungs for pneumonia, and he finally removed the cast from his leg. Dad's hair was now nearly two inches long and covered his head in a dark brown unruly thatch, accentuated by the white path where the stitches had been.

Each morning and evening Mom massaged Dad's arms and legs and moved them to maintain their flexibility. Although I could see no improvement, she insisted, daily, that he was getting better.

We rolled Dad onto his stomach, unkinked the lines, and Mom began to massage his back.

Unsmiling, she worked mechanically, kneading the sparse muscles and rubbing the thin skin.

I stood by, studying the sadness in her face. "Are you all right?" I asked somberly.

Her eyes lowered, Mom nodded her head silently;

then after a moment said forcefully, "Oh, Rob, what did I ever do to encourage that . . . that . . . old goat?"

I was glad the room was dark enough to hide the flush that sprang to my cheeks. "It's not your fault, Mom," I said in a shaky voice.

"He and Pauline seemed so helpful. Just good neighbors." Her voice trailed off as she continued to knead Dad's shoulders. "I never thought of him as anything but—"

"It's hard to understand," I ventured. I was embarrassed that we were having this conversation, especially with Dad lying there. My own hormones had begun to bubble, and my interest in girls had intensified during the past few months. But I was extremely uncomfortable to be seen as a confidant by my own mother.

Mom began flexing Dad's knee. "I've tried to think of anything I could have said or done that might have encouraged his . . . his . . . advance," she said, carefully choosing the word.

"Mom, it's not your fault," I repeated.

A low moan escaped Dad's throat as she continued flexing his leg. "I'm sorry, John," she said, "but it's got to be done. You don't want to be stiff when you wake up, do you?"

"Will he ever wake up?" I seized the opportunity to change the subject.

"Of course he will." She continued to bend his leg. "Soon." She massaged Dad's calf. After a moment she said more softly, "Rob, have faith. You have to have faith before any miracles occur."

"I'm sorry, Mom," I replied guiltily. "It's just that it has been a long time."

"Maybe we needed to be tested."

"Why?" I asked.

"I don't know. I'm not sure we ever know." Suddenly she straightened and turned toward me. In the dim lamp light I could see her smiling.

"Mom?"

"That's all it was, wasn't it, Rob?"

"Wasn't what?" I said wrinkling my brow.

"Gus. That's all it was. A test."

"I suppose," I said slowly.

She turned back to working with Dad's leg. "Thanks for your help, Rob."

I knew that I had been dismissed and was not sure why I had been thanked.

I made my way back to the living room and sat down next to Ginger on the couch. On the television set, four men in overalls were singing a song about Texaco gasoline. It seemed as if we were an ordinary family in an ordinary house on an ordinary night and there was comfort in the ordinariness of it all.

Ginger switched off the television set, then plopped back beside me on the couch.

"Rob?"

"What?"

"Are we ever going to open our Christmas presents?"

"Yes we are, Ginger," I replied. "Soon."

❀ 20 ❀

As Ginger and I climbed off the bus the next Friday, my heart leapt to my throat. A stack of fifty or so white plywood boxes sat in the driveway. Beehives. Unconsciously I rubbed my left cheek. It was as if I could feel the swelling still there. My eyelid flickered a tiny bit.

Three years before, when I was nine, I had been watching Dad place the beehives around the orchard, and a bee had stung me on my cheek. The pain was like fire, and I had run screaming into the house. Mom had teased the stinger out with a needle and applied a paste of baking soda to the site, but an hour later my cheek had swollen to the point that I could not open my eye. Then the chills began, with shivering that I could not control. Mom called Dr. MacArthur, who advised her to have me take a couple of aspirin and keep me bundled up. The next morning, when my fever still had not broken, Mom took me to the clinic.

"He's showing a fairly strong reaction to the sting," said Dr. MacArthur. "He'll be fine, but I'd keep him away from bees."

The shivering had stopped, and I was beginning to feel half human.

"Usually," continued the doctor, "subsequent stings bring even more violent reactions."

"I see," said Mom. "What does that mean, exactly?"

Dr. MacArthur pulled his stethoscope out of his ears and hung it around his neck. He toyed with the bell of it as he said, "It means, if he's stung many more times, it could be fatal."

My mother's face went white. "Fatal?"

"Elizabeth, just keep him away from bees. Okay?"

Since that day I had avoided bees at all costs. Now a huge stack of beehives lay in our driveway. Warily I tiptoed past them toward the front porch, opened the front door, and quickly closed it behind me. I leaned against the inside of the door, breathing heavily.

"Is that you, Rob?" Mom called from Dad's room.

"Yup," I said and walked quickly down the hall. Mom was massaging Dad's arm as I entered the room.

"I've done a terrible thing," she said.

"What?" I asked, trying to keep the alarm from my voice.

It seemed as if Mom was trying to avoid looking at me. "The bees," she said quietly.

"I saw them," I said, still panic stricken.

Mom worked silently for several moments. "I'm sure you understand why I can't turn to Gus for help," she finally said.

I nodded my head. And then I realized what Mom was saying. I was going to have to handle the beehives! Panic rose full blown in my heart. I felt as though I had been sucker-punched in the stomach.

"Isn't there anyone else . . . ?"

Slowly she shook her head. Finally she turned to me and sat down heavily on the chair beside the bed. "Sit down, Rob."

I sat. "What's wrong?"

"Rob, you know what went on between Gus and me."

I nodded my head.

"After the bees were delivered this morning, I called Pauline to see if she could suggest someone who might help with them."

"And?"

Mom inspected her hands for what seemed like a long time. Her shoulders shook slightly. "Oh, Rob, I'm not sure what Gus told her, but she made it clear we wouldn't be getting any help from them in the future."

"What did she say?" I could feel anger rising within me.

She waved her hand aimlessly in the air, "It doesn't matter."

"It does to me," I replied.

Mom stood up and started moving Dad's leg. In a whisper she finally said, "It seems that Pauline thinks I tried to get Gus to . . . oh, you know."

I wasn't sure that I did know, but I knew that not only was Uncle Gus a dirty old man, but he was a liar as well. My soul swelled with a righteous indignation coupled with a feeling of total helplessness.

"I don't know where else to turn, Rob," she continued. "But I do know the peaches are starting to blossom, and the pears, apples, and cherries won't be far behind. We've got to get the beehives into the orchard so the trees get pollinated."

"Mom . . ." I didn't want to reveal the terror that clung like a black spider on my heart . . . "I don't know enough about the bees. I don't know what we have to do . . . or how to do it." I stood and began pacing the room.

"Rob, we've both watched your father work the bees. I've had his books out all afternoon, and we can handle this."

I started to protest, but she stopped me with a shake of her head.

"Tomorrow we'll handle the bees." There was a sense of steel and finality in her voice.

"Mom, . . . I can't."

"Yes, you can, Rob. And I'll help."

Feebly I protested, but I knew I had lost the battle and that we would be dealing with the bees the next morning. I spent a sleepless night tossing and turning in my bed, trying to put down the mortal fear that churned within me.

After breakfast, Mom and I went down into the cellar and unpacked the bee equipment. I pulled on Dad's white coveralls that he used when he worked the bees. The cuffs on the pant legs hung eight inches past my feet. Mom helped me roll them up, then wrapped twine around them and cinched them tightly against my boots.

"That'll keep the bees out," Mom said, smiling.

I was still fighting the coldness in my stomach. "I hope so," I said gamely as I slid my hands into the gloves that reached past my elbows. The fingers were too big for my hands, but I could bend them clumsily.

Mom pulled the sleeves of the coveralls over the gloves, folded back the excess material, and slid rubber bands over the arrangement, sealing the opening to the cuffs. We climbed back up the cellar stairs to the kitchen, carrying the rest of the equipment. I could feel sweat coursing down my back.

"All you've got to do," Mom said, referring to a well-worn beekeepers' manual, "is put the base on the ground and then stack three supers on top of it."

Her forehead was wrinkled as she flipped back and forth through the book. "But I think we have to smoke the bees and then sprinkle some of this medicine into each section of the hive." She held up a quart mason jar full of white powder.

The sweat was running profusely down my back. "Mom," I whined, "are you sure we can do this?"

There was no hesitation, "Of course we can." She licked her thumb and searched through several more pages. "Put your hat on, and let's get started."

I adjusted the pith helmet on my head and pulled the bee veil down on my chest. A sweet smell of honey and beeswax enveloped me. Mom handed me a small, flat pry bar. I dropped it into my hip pocket.

"You'll need that hive tool to pry open the tops of the boxes," she said authoritatively.

Nearly swamped by Dad's coveralls and the too-large helmet and netting, I could feel myself trembling as I lumbered awkwardly toward the first stack of boxes. The buzzing of the bees was incessant as we approached the hives.

"Pick up a base," Mom directed. "Carry it over there." She pointed toward a couple of cinder blocks left from last year.

I picked up the square of plywood and placed it flat on the blocks. When I returned, Mom had already lighted a piece of burlap and placed it inside the smoker, a tin can that ended in a snout and had a bellows attached. Smoke drifted lazily out of the snout.

"Now carry one of the sections of hive over to the base," she directed. She looked into the book intently. "It's called a super."

I could hear the bees buzzing angrily inside the super as I picked it up, carried it to the waiting base, and set it down. The opening into the super had been plugged with a small wad of newspaper. As I set the super down, I could see the newspaper moving. Suddenly the news-paper was pushed out and a bee emerged, followed by a

stream of bees. They did not seem happy. I ran screaming back to where Mom was waiting in the driveway.

"What's wrong!" Mom cried out in alarm. "Did you
get stung!"

I realized that despite the flight of bees leaving the
hive, I had not been stung at all.

"They scared me," I said somewhat embarrassed.
"What do I do next?" trying to regain some dignity.

Mom screwed the lid off the bottle of medicine.
"Shoot some smoke into the hive, and then pry off the
top with the hive tool." She handed me the smoker.
"Then sprinkle a teaspoonful of this white powder on
top of the wooden frames inside the super."

I tried to absorb the directions. I nodded my head and
took the smoker in one hand and the mason jar in the
other. I could feel the hive tool in my pocket slapping
against my hip as I approached the beehive. Gingerly, I
placed the snout of the smoker next to the opening in
the hive and squeezed the bellows. A hearty puff of
smoke entered the hive. Immediately the sound of
buzzing changed. I waited a moment, set the smoker on
the ground, and reached into my hip pocket for the hive
tool. The bees had cemented the top of the super to the
sides with a sticky glue. I forced the blade of the hive
tool under the lid and pried it off. Stringy, dark brown

cobwebs stretched between the lid and the top of the box.

When I looked inside the super I could see the top edges of ten wooden frames hanging vertically inside the hive. The frames were covered with bees that were wiggling back and forth. Quickly I sprinkled a spoonful of white medicine on top of the frames and replaced the lid. I picked up the smoker and retreated to the driveway.

"What's next?" I said as nonchalantly as possible.

Mom studied the book for a few moments. "I think you just take another super out and stack it on top of the first one." She showed me a picture in the bee book.

With growing confidence I carried a second super out to the first, pried off the top again, and placed the second super on top of the first. Suddenly a cloud of bees surrounded me. I panicked and ran screaming back to the driveway. A number of bees were crawling on my veil, but as I approached Mom, one by one they flew away.

"Did you get stung?" Mom cried out in alarm.

"I'm all right," I said. "Just got a little spooked."

By late afternoon I had gotten into a pattern of carrying the individual pieces of the beehives to their resting spots, smoking the bees, treating them with medicine, and replacing the top of the hive. Mom had gone back in the house. I had learned that the bees could not sting me through the heavy clothing and had become quite nonchalant with the whole process. The sixteenth and final hive was close to the property line we shared with Gus and Pauline. As I carried the top super to its resting place, I could see Uncle Gus standing on his front porch, watching me. Defiantly, I stacked the hive in place and grabbed the smoker. After spooning in the medicine, I replaced the top and started back toward our house.

Sweat was rolling down my forehead and catching in my eyebrows. Halfway to the driveway, I pulled the helmet and veil from my head and wiped my brow with my gloved hand. At that moment a bee landed on my head. I felt it crawling through the sweat-soaked strands of hair. Instinctively, I slapped at it with my glove, crushing it. In a final frenzied act it stung me on the crown of my head. It felt as if a dagger had stabbed me. Despite the rubber bands securing the coveralls to my right glove, I succeeded in wrestling it off. Frantically I combed through my hair and plucked the remains of the bee off my head, while racing toward the house.

By the time I reached the kitchen door I felt as if the top of my head was on fire.

"Mom!" I screamed as I flung myself through the door. "I've been stung!"

She was kneading bread on the kitchen table. Quickly she dusted most of the flour from her hands on her apron and started searching through my hair. I sat down trembling on a kitchen chair. Dried flakes of dough rained down on my pants as Mom pawed the top of my head. Her hands were trembling almost as hard as mine.

"There it is," she said triumphantly. "Put your finger here, Rob." She grabbed my hand and marked the spot on my head with my finger. Quickly she searched in our kitchen junk drawer, found a pair of tweezers, and pulled the stinger from my head.

I was beginning to shake uncontrollably, while Mom made a paste of baking soda and spread it on my head. My breath was coming in ragged gasps.

"We've got to get you to the doctor," she said. She pulled me to my feet and supported me as we moved toward the front door. "Ginger," she called loudly.

"What?" my sister called from her room.

I could see the indecision in my mother's eyes. Dad lay unattended in his room; Ginger was only seven years old. I needed to get to the doctor. "Sweet Pea," Mom said steadily. "I need you to stay here with Dad while I run Rob to the doctor."

Ginger bounded down the stairs. "Are you going to be

gone long?" she asked, gnawing on the knuckle of her thumb.

Mom shook her head. "Just a few minutes. Are you going to be okay?"

"I guess," she said as she glanced down the hallway toward Dad's room.

I felt as though I couldn't breathe and was gasping more desperately for air.

"Ginger," Mom said urgently, "the doctor's number is written on the pad by the phone. You call if you have a problem. I've got to get Rob to the clinic." She pushed me out the front door.

❀ 21 ❀

MILLIE, DR. MACARTHUR'S receptionist,
took one look at me as Mom helped me wheezing
through the door and then rushed me past the half dozen
waiting patients to an examining room. Almost as soon
as I had lain down on the table, Dr. MacArthur burst
through the door. He listened to my labored breathing,
"What happened?"

"He was stung by a bee," Mom said with a shaky
voice. "You remember, he's allergic to bee stings."

I was still wearing Dad's white coveralls and the left
glove. "I need a bare arm," Dr. MacArthur said firmly,
reaching toward a glass cabinet. Mom pulled off the rubber band on my left hand, removed the glove, and

unbuttoned the front of the coveralls. I pulled my left arm out of the sleeve. I was struggling to breathe and was wide-eyed and thoroughly panicked.

Quickly Dr. MacArthur filled a hypodermic needle, rubbed my arm with an alcohol-soaked cotton ball, found a vein, and jabbed the needle into me. Within a few seconds I found that I could breathe more easily. The panic began to subside.

"That ought to take care of it," the doctor said as he pulled the needle from the syringe and dropped it into a stainless steel container of alcohol. He tore a strip of adhesive tape from a roll on the table and taped the cotton ball over the puncture in my arm. "What happened?"

Mom sniffled a little, then said, "Rob was putting the beehives out in the orchard. He was wearing all of our bee gear," she gestured at the coveralls and gloves, "but somehow a bee got to him."

Dr. MacArthur rubbed his chin. "Take off your shirt." He stuck his stethoscope in his ears. "Take a big breath." The cold metal bell pushed against my chest. He thumped me with the knuckle of his finger. "Another one." He listened to my chest and back. "You can put your shirt on," he said.

I buttoned my shirt and stuck my arm back into the

arm of the coveralls. With the rubber band removed, the sleeve hung six inches past my hand. I pushed it back up my arm so my hand extended.

The doctor leaned against the end of the examining table and tapped the bell of his stethoscope against the palm of his hand. "Elizabeth, this was a close one." He nodded his head. "You've got to keep this boy away from the bees. Understand?"

Meekly my mother nodded her head. "Mac, by next year John will be able to handle them. This year we had no choice."

"I thought Gus was helping you with the orchard," Dr. MacArthur said as he focused a small light in my right eye and peered into it. He took my wrist in his finger and probed for a pulse.

Mom looked at the floor near her feet. "He's been unable to help lately."

"Oh? Why?"

Mom shrugged her shoulders. "I'd rather not talk about it." Mom turned away from the doctor. "Anyway, John will be able to help us, soon."

He cleared his throat. "Elizabeth, can we speak frankly?"

"Of course."

"What if John doesn't recover?"

Mom rose quickly from her chair. "But he will, Mac, he will. He's getting better every day."

"Is he, Elizabeth?" Dr. MacArthur looked into my mother's eyes. I think that both of them had forgotten that I was there.

"Yes, he is," Mom said defiantly.

"Elizabeth, you know that I have been dropping by your house to check on your husband for weeks."

I was unaware that the doctor had been visiting so regularly.

He continued, "And in my professional opinion, John has not progressed at all since we let you take him home."

"But he is getting better. I can feel it," she replied in a voice so soft I could barely hear her. Then she dissolved into tears and began to sob, her whole frame shaking. She sank back onto the chair and buried her face in her hands. Dr. MacArthur put his hand protectively on her shoulder and let her cry.

"Elizabeth, perhaps we'd better wait until a better time," he said gently.

Mom shook her head. "Mac, I just know he's going to get better," she said through her sobs.

The doctor reached for his roll-around stool that stood next to the examining table. He plunked himself down on the green plastic top and inched himself to a spot in front of Mom. He reached out and took her hand. "Elizabeth, your husband has suffered and survived a massive skull fracture. He has been in a coma for more than three months. With every passing day there is less hope that he will ever recover consciousness."

Mom's shoulders continued to shake as she feebly shook her head.

"You are wearing yourself out," he continued. "You can't expect to run your farm by yourself." He glanced at me, "Even though you have your son to help you." He smiled a wan smile in my direction. "There are facilities that are equipped to handle those in John's condition until . . . well, you know."

Mom's sobbing stopped. Dr. MacArthur offered her a tissue from a blue and white box on his equipment stand. She blew her nose and wiped her eyes. "Thank you, Mac." She stood up and threw her hair back over her shoulders with a flip of her head. "We need to get home. Ginger is there taking care of her father. I certainly appreciate what you did for Rob. Please send me a bill." Her voice was cold and steady.

"Of course," the doctor said, rising from his stool and giving just the hint of a bow.

"Mac," my mother said, clenching her jaw, "I respect

your medical opinion. You've been a good friend, but you're wrong—dead wrong. John will recover. And he will recover at home." She pushed me ahead of her out of the examining room.

"Well, if anyone has the faith to make it happen, you do," replied the doctor as he held the door open for us.

We drove home in silence. As the car crunched into our driveway, I turned to Mom. "What if he doesn't get better?"

"I don't want to hear talk like that," she snapped. "Do you understand?"

I nodded my head. "But what if—"

"Rob," she said, the warning clear in her voice.

While I stripped off the coveralls and put away the bee gear in the cellar, Mom relieved Ginger of her vigil at Dad's bedside. When I climbed back up the stairs from the basement, Ginger was sitting on the couch in the front room. I sat down on the opposite end of the couch. We sat without speaking for a few moments.

"Ginger," I whispered.

"What?"

I looked around to make sure Mom was nowhere near.

"Do you think Dad's getting better?"

"I dunno. I guess so," she stammered. "What do you think?"

I shrugged my shoulders, stood up from the couch, and walked to the front window.

"Mom thinks so," I finally said.

Ginger looked at the stick that used to be our Christmas tree.

"Do you think we're ever going to open our presents?"

I knelt beside the remnants of the tree and replaced an ornament that had fallen from a bare branch.

"I hope so, Ginger."

❀ 22 ❀

I AWOKE THE NEXT morning and looked out my bedroom window, gazing toward the orchard. Overnight the peach trees had exploded into full bloom. A sea of pale pink extended as far as the eye could see. The sun was just climbing over the mountain, brushing the tops of the trees, making them glow a neon pink. Gingerly I touched the top of my head. The swelling had gone down, leaving a gumdrop-sized lump where the bee had stung me. The only other effect left was a terrible thirst. I hurried to the bathroom, turned on the cold water, and cupped my hand beneath it. Greedily I drank from my hand. When I came out of the bathroom, I could hear Mom puttering around downstairs in the kitchen.

"Morning, sleepyhead," she said as I walked yawning into the kitchen. "How do you feel?"

"I'm fine," I replied. Involuntarily my hand went to the lump on my head.

"That was scary," she said, turning to ladle some pancake batter into the frying pan on the stove.

"How's Dad?" I asked, trying to change the subject.

"He's fine," Mom said so quietly I could barely hear her across the kitchen. "He'll be fine."

We sat in silence for a long moment; then I asked, "Mom, what if Dr. MacArthur's right?"

"What do you mean?" she said tightly.

"Well, you know, what if Dad never gets better?"

Deftly she flipped the pancakes over with a spatula. "Rob," she said sternly, "he's wrong. Your father is getting better day by day."

I thought I could hear just a bit of doubt in her voice. "If you say so, Mom."

"Rob," she said, no doubt now evident. "Never give up hope. Now, go get your sister down here for breakfast." She waved the spatula in my direction.

"Ginger," I called from the bottom of the stairs, "breakfast's ready." There was no answer, so I climbed the stairs to Ginger's room. I pushed open her door. Her sheet and blanket were half on the floor, and she was curled up around her pillow near the bottom of her bed. Gently I shook her.

"Ginger."

She jerked violently, and her eyes flew open. She blinked them quickly, "Oh, Rob," she said, "I had the most terrible dream."

"Really?"

"Uh-huh, there were bees all over the place, and you were being stung, and Mom was trying to swat them, and she was being stung, and Dad was trying to get out of bed, but his plastic tubes were wrapped all around him." She paused for a breath, "And I was trying to help, but I couldn't move fast enough to help any of you."

Her face was white, and I could tell she was still living part of the dream.

"It was just a dream," I said flatly. "Don't think about it anymore."

"I don't want to, but it keeps coming back."

"Breakfast is ready," I said a little gruffly. "Hurry down. Mom's made pancakes."

"I'll hurry," she said and scurried toward the bathroom.

I descended the stairs slowly, aware that Ginger's dream had awakened a fear deep within me. I detoured to Dad's room before heading to the kitchen for breakfast. He lay as he had when he'd first come home from the hospital. His mouth was slightly open, and a dribble of saliva had dried on his chin. I realized that it was easier to help Mom turn him in bed now than it had been at first. He was losing weight, but other than that, I saw no change. If only I had my mother's faith. My eyes filled with tears as I stood looking at my father tethered to his life-sustaining tubing.

"Come and eat, Rob," my mother called from the kitchen.

I touched my father's cheek before joining Ginger and my mother for breakfast.

"Have you seen the orchard?" Mom asked as we sat down at the table. "I don't think the peaches have ever been so beautiful."

I nodded my agreement with my mouth full of pancake.

"Let's go see," Ginger said, hopping off her chair.

"After breakfast," said Mom. "They'll wait."

After the dishes were washed and dried, the three of us wandered out the back door into the orchard. The sun shone down through the pink cloud of peach blossoms. A subtle, heady perfume filled the mild air. The sky was pale blue and uncluttered by clouds. In short, it was a perfect spring morning. Ginger began dancing in slow circles at the margin of the orchard.

My mother looked upward and reverently said, "Thank you, Lord, for all the beauty you have given us." She paused, then continued, "And for all you have blessed us with." She swept her arms open wide, and years dropped from my mother until she looked like a young girl. She joined Ginger in a swirling dance in the orchard.

A smile lit my face, and I began walking toward them until I heard a sound that stopped me as surely as if I had run into a brick wall. The buzzing of bees! I focused on the blossoms of the nearest peach tree and saw an army of bees busy gathering nectar and pollinating the fruit. A river of cold sweat streamed down my back as I turned and ran toward the safety of the house.

"What's wrong?" my mother called after me.

"Bees," I yelled without breaking stride.

My mother sprinted after me into the kitchen. Her face was white. "Were you stung?" she asked frantically.

I shook my head, "No! But the trees are full of bees!"

"Thank goodness," she exhaled. "I was afraid . . ." she sank onto a chair.

I turned on the kitchen faucet and gulped cold water.

"I'm okay," I said, but my heart was thumping so vigorously I thought it must be visible through my shirt.

Taking a deep breath, I said, "Mom, next year I can't do the bees."

She heard the tremor in my voice. "You won't have to, Rob. Dad will do it."

23

CLOSE ON THE HEELS of the peaches, the apples and pears burst into bloom. Each day as Ginger and I arrived home from school we'd be bathed in the perfume of a thousand trees in blossom. The last three weeks of March were unseasonably warm and uncharacteristically devoid of rain. And then, perhaps as an April Fools' joke, the heavens opened up and flooded the orchard.

Mom had been inspecting the peaches and found a multitude of furry little mouse ears that would grow into our life-sustaining crop of fruit. I stayed as far away from the trees and bees as possible. With the rains, Mom stayed inside. The soft, loamy soil between the trees sucked shoes from your feet as you sank into the cocoa-colored mud.

Ginger's ceiling began to leak again. The drip was slower and mostly ran down the sloping ceiling to the west wall of her room where it collected on the floor next to the window. Mom mopped it up periodically with a dish rag that she would wring out into a bucket.

"Mom," Ginger asked, "are we going to have someone come and fix the roof?"

My mother finished wiping up the water and pushed herself to her feet. "Sometime, Sweet Pea," she said, pushing strands of hair out of her face with the back of her hand. "Right now, money's a little tight."

I realized I had not worried about our finances at all. With last year's bumper crop, I had the feeling that we had plenty of money to see us through the year.

"What do you mean?" I asked timidly.

"Oh, nothing, Rob," she said twisting her mouth so she could blow a strand of hair off her cheek. "We'll be fine."

"I thought last year was a good year," I exclaimed.

Mom picked up the bucket of water and carried it toward the bathroom. "It was, son," she said, "but your father's medical expenses have been more than I'd counted on." She dumped the water into the toilet. "But we'll be fine. It looks like another good crop."

My mother went back to Ginger's room, and I made my way down to the front room. I curled up on the couch and watched the windblown rain beat against the windows. The Christmas stick stood silently, the ornaments shining dully in the gray afternoon light. As the needles continued to fall, Ginger had pushed the presents farther under the tree. The scene evoked a feeling of melancholy, and my spirits sank. I rested my elbow on the arm of the couch and nestled my chin in the palm of my hand. At that moment I could think of no single thing in my life that offered joy. We had not been a very religious family. At least, we rarely attended church. But my mother's faith had instilled in me a belief in God. In that moment of total despair, I closed my eyes and called out from the depths of my soul, "Lord, what have we done to deserve this?" I could feel tears squeezing out of the corners of my eyes. "How long do we have to endure this?"

The rain beat on the panes with an increased fury.

"I know we're not supposed to ask for a sign, but I need one. Anything. I'm just a boy. I don't know how much more I can take. Please, Lord."

Suddenly the wind stopped, and as I opened my eyes,

a single ray of sunlight broke through the clouds and illu-minated the Christmas tree. A single silver ornament caught the light and sent it dancing across the wall and ceiling, and at that moment the weight was lifted and I somehow felt that everything was going to be all right.

Within a few moments the clouds began to clear, and the orchard was bathed in sunlight. The petals of the pollinated blossoms had been washed from the trees in the downpour, and the bright pinkness had been replaced by a haze of golden green created by the tiny leaves that had emerged. I listened to the last drops of rain dripping from the eaves in an uneven pattern around the house. Then Mom came down the stairs.

"Looks like the storm's broken up," she said with a smile on her face. "At least the drip in Ginger's room has stopped." She started down the hallway toward Dad's room, and I followed her with a bounce in my step.

The IV bottle was nearly empty, and Mom deftly replaced it with a full one from the stock next to his bed. The two of us turned him over, and Mom made sure his mouth and nose weren't blocked by his pillow.

"Mom," I said cheerfully, "Dad is getting better."

"Of course he is," she said. "Was there any doubt?"

Timidly I scratched my foot on the floor. "I could get a job after school."

"What?"

"I could help out with some money," I said. "They're always looking for bag boys at the market."

"Rob, you're already doing more than I could ever hope for. You've taken care of the furnace, you've pruned the orchard." Tears misted her eyes, "You've even set out the beehives," she said with a shudder.

"I could still help earn some money," I said with a slight smile.

Mom shook her head. "We'll be fine. You'll see."

"I know we will," I said, suppressing a grin.

Mom stared at me quizzically. "You seem awfully chipper," she said.

I nodded my head. I wanted to share the experience I had just felt, but I was afraid she would find it silly. Embarrassed, I just smiled.

❀ 24 ❀

By the end of the week the cherries were in full bloom. Their snow-white blossoms had exploded like popcorn covering their branches. The bees hummed a steady buzz among the flowers, providing a constant reminder for me to stay a respectable distance from the trees as I inspected the orchard. Dad and I will have to top some of those trees next year, I thought as I looked at the trees through different eyes. Though it was true the orchard had changed as the cherry trees grew taller, the greater change had come in me. A feeling of oneness with the land had begun to blossom in my heart.

When I reached the far border of our land, I spent some time inspecting the irrigation gate, knowing that in a couple of weeks our watering turns would begin and I would have to know how to open the gate and direct the water down the furrows. A bright, new padlock secured the rusted chain that ran through the wheel that opened the gate. *I wonder where that came from*, I thought, *I'll have to get a key before I can irrigate the fields*. Staying well away from the bees in the cherries, I whistled my way back home through the orchard.

Mom was busily working at her sewing machine when I walked through the kitchen door. Only the year before, Dad had replaced her old treadle-driven machine with a sleek, black Singer with an electric motor. Mom hummed softly as she fed fabric under the pressure foot of the machine.

"Whatcha' making?" I asked.

Surprised, she jumped a little. Color rose in her cheeks, and she pulled a cluster of pins from between her lips. "Oh, Rob. You startled me. It's a surprise for Ginger. A new dress. Next Sunday is Easter, you know."

I nodded my head while a smile lit up my face. Easter meant hidden baskets full of candy.

"I thought we'd color some eggs next Saturday," she said while the sewing machine continued to hum. Then, almost as an afterthought, she said, "Would you check to make sure we have some vinegar?"

We generally had a gallon bottle of Heinz white vine-gar stored underneath the kitchen sink. I opened the cupboard door and quickly spied it near the back wall. It was about half full.

"We've got plenty," I said. We colored eggs by adding a color tablet to a teaspoon of vinegar in a teacup full of hot water.

"Where's Ginger?" I asked.

"I sent her over to Pauline's with some cookies," she said without taking her eyes off her sewing. "Sort of a peace offering."

"Oh."

"Besides, I figured it would get her out of the house while I worked on her dress. There are more cookies in the jar." She nodded toward the cookie jar on the counter.

I fished a cookie out of the jar—oatmeal with raisins, my favorite. Contentedly I perched on the corner of the table and nibbled on the cookie. "Mom, do you know who put a padlock on the irrigation gate?"

She shook her head. "I haven't an idea. I haven't been back there to look at it since last summer. Your father always took care of that chore. Maybe your dad has a key on his key ring."

"It looked brand new," I said through my mouthful of cookie.

"When I get through here, I'll call Pete down at the irrigation company," she said, putting more pins between her lips. "He can probably get us a key."

I snagged another cookie, "Okay, our first watering turn is on the fifteenth, I think."

Mom nodded as the sewing machine whirred. She worked the dress material back and forth, then stopped the needle and snipped the thread with a pair of scissors. "There." She held the finished dress for me to see. "What do you think?"

"Looks real pretty," I replied.

"Do you think Ginger will like it?"

I nodded my head. "Sure."

We heard the front door open. Quickly Mom placed the dress on a hanger and hung it out of sight on the mud porch. "That you, Sweet Pea?"

Solemn faced, Ginger walked into the kitchen. She was carrying the plate of cookies in her hands. It was plain that she had been crying.

"What's the matter?" Mom said, dropping to one knee beside Ginger.

Ginger struggled to hold back the tears. "Aunt Pauline wasn't home," she said haltingly, "and Uncle

Gus told me to get off their property." She sniffled. "Mom, what did I do wrong?"

Mom took the plate of cookies and set it on the counter before enveloping Ginger in a hug. "Nothing, Sweet Pea, nothing at all. Don't you worry about it." She held Ginger's face between her hands and rubbed the tears off her cheeks with her thumbs. "That means we'll have more cookies for ourselves. Rob, would you get some glasses out of the cupboard?"

"Sure."

Mom filled the tumblers with milk, and we sat around the kitchen table munching cookies. The telephone rang, and Mom leaned back in her chair and grabbed the receiver. "Hello?"

She listened without saying another word and then slammed the receiver back on its cradle. I could see the color rising in her neck and cheeks. Her jaw was set, and abruptly she shoved her chair back and stomped out of the kitchen.

I looked at Ginger and shrugged my shoulders. "Beats me," I said as I pushed my chair back and followed Mom down the hallway to Dad's room. She had pulled their nightstand drawer open and was thumbing through a stack of papers. Abruptly she held up a single sheet and stepped to the window to take advantage of the afternoon light. She scanned the document and then stomped back down the hallway to the kitchen.

Ginger was still sitting at the table munching on a cookie. Mom grabbed the telephone and waited for the operator to answer. "Wilma, I need to talk to Pete Crenshaw at the water district." There was a brief response. "I know it's Saturday; I just hope he's there." Mom tapped her fingers on the kitchen counter while she waited for the call to be put through.

"Pete, this is Elizabeth Henderson. I'm glad you're there." She paused, "Just fine. He's getting better every day." Another pause. "Pete, I just had a call from Gus Rogers with some baloney about our irrigation water." She waited again, occasionally uttering an "uh-huh" as she listened to the man from the water district. Her fingers drummed even more insistently on the counter.

"I see," she finally said. "How much longer are you going to be there?" She waited for the response. "Much obliged, I'll be right down." There was another brief response from Pete, and then Mom said, "Thank you. Good-bye." She hung up the phone.

"I've got to run into town," she said.

"What's the matter?"

"Nothing," she said. But I could see the muscles in her jaw flexing.

"Mom," I pled, "what's wrong?"

She slipped her coat on and grabbed her purse. "Apparently our irrigation water bill hasn't been paid. If I don't get a check down to the water district, in the next fifteen minutes, your dear Uncle Gus will own our share." With that she stormed out the back door.

The tires peppered the shed with gravel as Mom gunned the car out of the driveway. I looked down the road to where our mailbox and Uncle Gus's shared a support halfway between our two houses. In a flash I knew who had put the new padlock on the irrigation gate. *How could a man who had done so much for us be so mean?* I wondered.

MOM RETURNED HOME less than half an hour later. The anger and tenseness I had seen in her when she left was gone. "Everything okay?" I asked as she walked back into the kitchen.

"Just fine," she said, with a slight smile on her face.

Ginger had wandered into the living room and was watching *Hopalong Cassidy* on the television set. "Are you all right?" I asked again.

"I'm fine," she said. "I'm sorry I let that old goat get to me." She hung up her coat and tucked her purse into its usual corner on the kitchen counter under the cupboards.

"Mom, you didn't do anything wrong. I mean, it was

Uncle Gus who . . ." I could feel my face beginning to burn. "Well, you know."

Mom's face became very serious.

"Rob, sometimes when we try to justify our actions we fool ourselves and shift the blame from where it belongs. I don't know what's going through that old fool's head, but I do know that he's not going to make me lose my temper again."

She picked up the plate of cookies that Ginger had left on the counter. "Will you look after Dad for a few more minutes? I shouldn't have sent a girl to do a woman's work."

"Where are you going?" I asked, although I knew.

"To kill an old coot with kindness." She tugged her coat back on. "I'll be back soon." Carrying the plate of cookies, she went out through the kitchen door.

I joined Ginger in the living room, where the black-clad Hoppy had just ridden into town on Topper. Ginger was sitting on the floor in front of the television set, holding a half-eaten cookie and a half-empty glass of milk in her hands. She was staring at the show, completely involved in the episode. I noticed that another ornament had fallen off the Christmas tree onto the pile of faded packages, and I hung it on one of the bare branches before trying to get involved in the television program. Apparently the bad guys were trying to blow up a pass with dynamite, but Windy, Hoppy's sidekick, had overheard the plan.

Balancing her cookie and half-empty glass of milk, Ginger scooted backwards across the floor and leaned her back against the couch. Her eyes were glued to the small screen as the desperadoes set the dynamite charge. Hopalong and Windy diverted the cattle at the last minute before an explosion closed the pass. We were watching so closely that I barely heard the kitchen door open and close. Mom walked into the living room and perched on the arm of the couch.

"Pretty exciting," she said, gesturing toward the television.

"How did things go?" I asked, noticing that she did not have the plate of cookies with her.

She looked vacantly at the Christmas tree. "He's a stubborn old man, Rob, but at least he can't blame me for not trying."

"What happened?"

"I took them the cookies, and both of them told me to leave." Mom's brow wrinkled a little. "So I left the plate of cookies on their porch." She looked at me and smiled a gentle smile. "Oh, and one other thing. I told him to get that padlock off the irrigation gate first thing in the morning."

"And?"

"I guess we'll just have to see." She rose from the couch. "I'm going to check on your father," she said, stepping lightly into the hallway.

As a commercial for Ipana toothpaste flashed on the screen, Ginger scooted back across the floor and turned off the television set. Then, still on her knees, she reached to finger the wrapping paper on one of the presents. The brittle paper tore a little where her finger caught on a crease. She sighed.

Because of the cookies, none of us were very hungry, and we ate dinner later than usual. As soon as Ginger and I finished the dishes, I said goodnight and climbed up the stairs to go to bed. With the lights out, I sat on the edge of my bed and rested my elbows on the windowsill. In the moonlight I could see the incandescent glow of the cherry blossoms through my bedroom window. If the bees continued to do their work, it appeared we'd have another bumper crop of fruit. I found that thought both comforting and disquieting.

Another good crop would solve our financial woes, but how we would ever get the trees sprayed, the fruit picked, packed, and shipped to market without Dad's help, I didn't know. *Why can't life be easier?* I wondered as I lay back on my bed with my hands beneath my head. Sleep came slowly.

The Sunday morning sun beamed through the window into my face. I rolled over and tried to go back to sleep, but it was no use. I slipped out of bed and got dressed. Mom was already in the kitchen making breakfast.

"Morning, Rob," she said as I wandered in, rubbing the sleep from my eyes.

"Morning."

"After breakfast would you go check the head gate and make sure that padlock's gone?"

"Sure," I said stretching and yawning.

Ginger trailed me into the kitchen. "Can I go, too?"

"Of course," Mom said. "Make sure you put on your boots; it's still a little muddy in the orchard."

When breakfast was finished, the two of us walked through the orchard toward the irrigation gate. The bees obviously did not know that Sunday was a day of rest; they were buzzing loudly, and I detoured away from the cherries to the peaches, where the fruit was already forming into marble sized, green, fuzzy nuggets. Ginger clomped after me. In the distance a dog howled a mournful tune as we approached the head gate. The padlock was gone. I turned to start back to the house.

"Is that all we came to see?" asked Ginger.

"Yup. Had to make sure we can take our water turn."

Ginger lowered her head and followed me back to the house. There on the back porch was an empty cookie plate.

❦ 26 ❦

THAT AFTERNOON the phone rang insistently as Mom and I were turning Dad in his bed. There are those who would disagree, who think the phone always sounds the same, but I think there are moments when it fairly screams for attention.

"Ginger, get the phone," Mom called down the hall-way.

The phone rang a couple more times. Then we heard Ginger's muted, "Hello?"

Mom began flexing Dad's leg, massaging it as she did.

"Mom, it's for you," Ginger called.

Reluctantly Mom lowered Dad's leg, then hurried to the kitchen. I began to rearrange Dad's sheets around his emaciated frame when I heard Mom's voice from the kitchen. "I'll be right there!" I could tell something was wrong.

"Rob, I've got to run over to Pauline's. Take care of things." She was gathering her coat and her purse as she spoke.

"What's wrong?"

"There's been an accident. I've got to help Pauline get Gus to the doctor."

"What happened?"

"I'm not sure. I've got to hurry. I'll tell you when I get back." And she was out the door.

Ginger and I stood watching through the open kitchen door as Mom wheeled the speeding car down our graveled driveway toward the main road.

"Where's Mom going?" Ginger asked.

"Uncle Gus had an accident," I replied. "I don't know much more." I led her into the living room. The remnant of sunset bathed the room in ruby rays.

"How long is Mom going to be gone?" asked Ginger.

"Not too long, I hope."

The clock on the mantle chimed its hollow tone. Ginger burrowed into one corner of the couch. "Can we watch Ed Sullivan?"

"Sure," I said, twisting the knob on the front of the

television set. The yellow, cyclopean eye opened, and we hypnotically watched the show. As the final act was ending, we saw the flash of headlights through the front window and heard the crunch of gravel in the driveway. A few moments later Mom opened the kitchen door.

"How's Uncle Gus?" I asked as Mom entered the living room.

Her face was white, tinged yellow by the flickering light of the television set. "Not too good," she said somberly.

"What happened?"

Mom removed her coat and hung it up in the hall closet. "Apparently Gus was working on his truck. You know how much trouble that carburetor has given him."

I nodded my head.

"Anyway, he must have been cleaning some parts or something in gasoline. Apparently the gas fumes ignited, and the whole thing exploded in his face." Her hands were trembling badly. "His face is pretty badly burned, and he's in a lot of pain." Tears were spilling down her cheeks. "And his hands . . ." Her voice trailed off.

"Is he going to be all right?"

She nodded her head slightly. "They think so. They hope so. They've taken him into the hospital. They did all that they could at the clinic. They mostly treated the pain; then they sent him in an ambulance. Pauline went with him."

Three-month-old memories of the ambulance pulling out of our front yard flooded my head.

Mom sank down on the arm of the couch. She shook her head. She was crying.

"What is it, Mom?"

Her shoulders shook while she tried to regain her composure. After a moment she said, "That day, when I took the cookies over . . ." she looked at me, her face a mask of pain.

I nodded my head, uncomfortable in the role of confidant.

"Gus demanded that I get off their property."

"So?"

Her shoulders shook again; then she took a deep breath and looked at the ceiling. "I told him he could yell all he wanted, but that as far as I was concerned I had nothing to be ashamed of and he could burn in hell for all I cared. 'Burn in hell,' Rob. That's what I said."

I stood in front of my mother and put my hands on her shoulders. "Mom, you didn't have anything to do with this. You can't blame yourself."

"Oh, I know it's silly," she said shaking her head slowly from side to side. "But why did I have to use those words?" She wiped the tears from her cheeks with the back of her hand.

"It's good you were here to help," I said, trying to calm her down.

"Just 'cause Pauline's never learned to drive."

"Mom, you're not to blame." I said it with as much emphasis as I could.

She rose slowly and walked down the hall to Dad's room. I followed her silently. She knelt down beside my father's bed and rested her face against his arm.

"John," she said in muffled tones, "I need you."

In the kitchen the telephone rang. I ran down the hall and answered it on the second ring.

"Hello?"

"Rob, this is Aunt Pauline." Her voice was shaky.

"How's Uncle Gus?" I asked.

"They've taken him into surgery. I promised your mother I'd call her as soon as we knew anything. Is she there?"

"Just a minute," I said. I covered the mouthpiece with my hand and called, "Mom, it's Aunt Pauline." I spoke back into the phone. "She'll be here in a minute."

"Thank you," she said, her voice sounding tired and weak.

My mother took the telephone from me. "Pauline,

how is he?" she asked. Although I stood next to Mom, I couldn't hear Aunt Pauline's reply, but I saw relief flood Mom's face.

"But that's good, Pauline," she said softly. "How long do they think?"

I left my mother and went back into the living room. Ginger was still watching television. I stood beside the remnant of the Christmas tree and gazed out the window into the blackness of the night. I had not told my mother that I had been wishing, perhaps praying, for some sort of retribution for Uncle Gus and twinges of guilt were nipping at my soul.

"She's pretty sure he's going to be all right," Mom said as she walked into the living room. "He'll have some scars on his face, but he should have full use of his hands. He was lucky." She smiled a wan, little smile in my direction.

"Mom," I said quietly, "isn't it funny that it took something like this to break down the wall between our two families?"

"God moves in mysterious ways, Rob."

❧ 27 ❧

T HE WEEK CREPT ON toward Easter break. Early
each morning, before the school bus came, Mom would
drive Aunt Pauline to the hospital while Ginger and I
watched Dad and then, in the evening, after dinner,
Mom would drive back to bring her home. There was
hope that Uncle Gus could come home by the end of the
week.

Thursday we finished our last assignments before the
holiday and tossed our books into our lockers. Mr.
Fletcher dropped us off in front of our house. "See ya in
a week," he waved as the door shushed closed behind us.
We waved in return and crunched down the driveway to
our house. Behind the house the cherry trees continued

to display their brilliant whiteness, the subtle perfume of their blossoms filling the air.

Mom was waiting in the kitchen as Ginger and I entered the house, where the tantalizing odor of simmering stew made our mouths water.

"I'm going to run over to the hospital and pick up Pauline," she said. "Dinner's on the stove, and we'll eat as soon as I get back. Keep an eye on your father, okay?"

"Can I go with you?" Ginger asked in a whiny voice.

"If you put on a happy face," Mom said smiling.

"Can I go?" Ginger said, all sweetness and light.

"Come on, Sweet Pea. Rob, you'll be all right, won't you?"

"Sure, Mom," I replied.

She and Ginger disappeared out the kitchen door, and I heard the car pull out of the driveway. I opened the refrigerator and rummaged around for a snack to hold me for an hour. I settled on a glass of milk and a handful of cookies from the cookie jar.

A quick glance told me Dad lay thin and unchanged. I climbed to my bedroom and looked out over the orchard. Weeds were beginning to grow in the rows between the trees. *Time to get out on the tractor,* I thought. Dad had let me drive it a few times the last couple of years, and I believed I could handle it.

I finished the cookies and milk, returned to the kitchen, and washed out the glass. Then I went to sit with Dad. The afternoon sun reflecting from the cherry blossoms cast a glow on his pale face. He looked completely at peace. I didn't know whether he could hear me, but I felt the need to talk to him.

"Dad," I said barely above a whisper, "I love you." I realized I had not told him that in several years and experienced a sudden rush of emotion. After a moment, I went on. "You've taken such good care of us. I never realized how much you did for us until I had to do part of it." I reached out and took his hand in mine. His skin felt dry and fragile, as fragile as the wrapping paper on our Christmas gifts.

I looked out the window. "Lord, I don't know if I'll ever walk through our orchard again with my father, but I need to thank you for the years we've had together."

I stroked Dad's hand, "And, Dad, if you get better," I paused. "No! *When* you get better, you can count on me to help with the chores without complaining."

I'm not sure when the tears began falling, but I was sniffling, wiping my nose with one hand while holding my father's hand with the other. Despite my tears, there was a comfortable feeling in the room as the light faded in increments as tiny as the movement of the minute hand on the clock. I closed my eyes for what I thought was a moment, but when I opened them again, the room was growing dark. In spite of the advancing twilight, my dad's face had an almost luminous glow as he lay there, helpless, the nearly imperceptible drip traveling down the lifeline attached to his other hand, all that was sustaining his life.

I heard the car pull into the driveway and ran upstairs to the bathroom to wash my face. Mom and Ginger opened the back door. "We're home," Mom called cheerfully. "How's Dad?"

"Just fine," I called down the stairs. "How's Uncle Gus?"

"Might be able to come home on Saturday," she replied as she hung up her coat. "They'll remove the bandages from his face tomorrow, and then we'll know if he can come home. Pauline's hopeful."

"Mom, I'm hungry," Ginger complained.

"Well, put some bowls on, and we'll have dinner."

A few minutes later we sat down at the table. Uncharacteristically, Mom bowed her head. "Let's say grace," she said. "Lord, thank you for all that you have blessed us with. We have so much to be thankful for. Please forgive us of our weaknesses and our lack of faith.

Strengthen us for what lies ahead. And please bless this food. Amen."

A chill ran down my spine. "Mom, what do you think lies ahead?" I asked.

"I don't know, Rob. But whatever it is, we can handle it." She ladled stew into my bowl and handed it to me.

We were silent for a moment; then I said, "Tomorrow morning I think I'm going to get the tractor out and knock down the weeds in the orchard." I waited for her response.

Mom handed Ginger a bowl of stew. The only reaction I could see was that her left eyebrow rose slightly before she looked me straight in the eye. "If you think it needs to be done, go ahead."

28

I'M TAKING PAULINE over to the hospital," Mom said as she slid the plate of French toast in front of me. "Wait till I get back to plow the orchard, okay?"

"Mom, I'll be fine," I said as I bit into a maple-syrup-soaked square of toast.

"I'm not doubting you, Rob, but I need you to keep an eye on your father while I'm gone."

I nodded my head, and Mom grabbed the car keys from the hook by the kitchen door. Ginger slid a piece of French toast around her plate with her fork, soaking up syrup as she went. She popped the morsel into her mouth, leaving a track of syrup drops down the front of her nightgown.

"It seems like Saturday," she said as she dabbed at the syrup with a moistened finger.

"Nice to have a vacation," I said, glancing out the window. "But I think I'm going to have plenty to do to keep busy." I reached over to the sink and grabbed the wet dishrag. "Here, use this to get the syrup off." I handed it to Ginger. The cold moistness of the cloth caused her to inhale.

"That's cold," she complained.

"Sorry," I smiled.

"Rob, I had another dream," she said shyly.

"Oh?"

"It was Christmas, and we were all sitting in the living room. All of us, you and me and Mom and Dad. And it was snowing, and we were opening our presents."

"Sounds nice."

Ginger smiled. "It was. And the funny thing was we were opening the presents that are under the tree." She motioned with her head toward the living room.

"What else?" I asked.

She shook her head, "Nothing. That's all. But it felt really good."

I smiled at my little sister. Her hair was matted, and she had syrup on her chin. "Well, let's hope we don't have to wait until next winter. Why don't you go wash up and get dressed while I do the dishes; then we can play a game until Mom gets home." Ginger hopped down from her chair and carried her plate to the counter next to the sink.

"I'll finish the dishes and then check on Dad. Pick out a game."

Dad lay uncomplaining in his bed. I patted his hand gently. "Today I'm going to plow the orchard," I whispered.

Ginger had brought a picture puzzle down to the living room. The puzzle had a hundred pieces and was a picture of two small black-and-white puppies. "Can we do the puzzle? Please, Rob."

"Let me set up the table," I replied. The card table was folded up and stored on the back porch. I brought it into the living room and unfolded the legs. We dumped the puzzle pieces onto the table and turned them so that all the picture sides were up. Ginger began hoarding the border pieces in front of her.

It took only a few minutes to complete the puzzle. When it was done, Ginger began to put it back in the box, taking care to keep some of the pieces hooked together, but I made her scramble them up.

"Want to play Chutes and Ladders?" Ginger asked.

"Sure," I replied. She ran upstairs with the puzzle box

and returned quickly with the game. We played Chutes and Ladders for a long time, and Mom had still not returned home. I checked on Dad again. Nothing had changed.

"Want to play Candy Land?" Ginger asked.

"Sure." While I had been checking on Dad, Ginger had brought the new game to the table. We unfolded the game board.

"I want to be red," she said, reaching for a game piece.

We had just finished the third game when Mom pulled into the driveway. "I've got to get ready to plow the orchard," I said rather proudly to Ginger.

"Can I ride on the tractor with you?" she asked.

"I don't think so," I replied. Just then the kitchen door opened, and a moment later Mom walked slowly into the living room.

"How's Uncle Gus?" I said; then I saw the look on my mother's face. "What's wrong?"

Mom sank onto the couch. She was holding her hand to her mouth. After a moment she looked at me.

"He's blind," she whispered.

"What?"

"They took the dressings off his face, and he can't see." She turned her eyes to the window, staring without seeing. "They didn't think his eyes were affected when they treated his face, but . . ."

"Is he still coming home tomorrow?" I said. As soon as I asked, I felt that it was a foolish question.

"What?" Mom blinked her eyes and seemed to awaken from a trance.

"Nothing," I said.

"I feel so sorry for him," Mom continued. "His hands wrapped in gauze and bandages, his face so badly scarred, and now this." She drew her legs up under her and sat huddled in the corner of the couch.

I felt totally and completely helpless. Part of me wanted to comfort my mother, but a deeper, more primal self wanted to escape. "I'm going out to plow the orchard," I said weakly.

Mom nodded her head, and I went out to the garage and climbed onto the seat of the tractor. The ignition key had long ago been lost, replaced by a couple of pieces of wire. I touched them together, and the engine cranked like an old man waking from a winter's sleep. Just as I began to fear the battery was going to give out, the engine chuffed into life, belching a plume of black smoke out the stack. While the engine idled, I checked the hydraulic lift and locked the plow tines into place. Slowly I lifted them off the ground, pulled the throttle lever down a little, shifted into gear, and the tractor lurched forward out of the garage.

I swung around the edge of the house and aimed for the far corner of the orchard. The tractor bucked through the irrigation ditch, nearly bouncing me off the seat, but once I was into the orchard, the ground smoothed out, and I made my way quickly through the trees. When I reached the southwest corner of our property, I slowed to a stop, then turned the tractor and aimed it down the first row between the apple trees. Small green fruit covered the branches. I tugged on the hydraulic lever and dropped the tines of the plow to the ground. Carefully I maneuvered the tractor between the trees, scraping furrows in the earth behind me. Nervous about snagging the trees, I drove slowly, the odor of fresh-turned soil swirling around me. When I reached the end of the row, I lifted the plow, made a turn, and began the next row. As I finished the fifth row, I saw Mom standing behind the house watching me plow. I stopped the tractor, climbed off, and walked to where she stood.

"You're doing a good job, son," she said with pride in her voice.

I gave her a brief nod. "I'd better get on with it,"

I said. By the time I finished the next two rows, she had gone back into the house.

Three hours later I had finished plowing our orchard and was looking it over proudly, when through the trees I saw Miss Steenblick, the county nurse, backing her car out of our driveway. Mom's right, I thought, we can handle this. I started the tractor once more and drove down the east property line toward the house. I noticed the weeds that were growing between the trees on the other side of the fence in Uncle Gus's orchard. At first a certain smugness rose within me, but then I thought of him scarred and blind. When I got to the end of our lot, instead of pulling into our garage, I turned onto his property and began plowing Uncle Gus's orchard.

❀ 29 ❀

THE NEXT MORNING Mom left early to take Aunt Pauline to the hospital. A distant rumble of thunder hinted of possible rain later in the day, although few clouds were evident. I had not slept particularly well. My head was filled with the satisfaction of getting the orchard plowed but also the troubling revelation that Uncle Gus was blind. I had tossed and turned, mixing phantoms and fantasy with reality.

I sat down in the chair next to Dad's bed and reached out and patted him gently on his shoulder. Although Mom had tried to comb his hair, it stuck out like porcupine quills with a white track leading around the back of his head.

"Dad," I said gently, "I got the orchard plowed yesterday. It looks pretty good. I think you'd be happy." I reached out and stroked his hand. "Uncle Gus had an accident." I didn't know whether Mom had told him, or if she had, whether he had heard. "His truck carburetor blew up in his face." I paused to see if there was any reaction. There was not. "Dad, he's blind." Still no reaction. "I plowed his orchard yesterday. I hope that was all right."

Thunder rumbled again in the distance. I arose, went to the window, and opened it slightly. The mingled fragrance of new-turned earth and cherry blossoms washed through the room, filling every corner.

"Dad," I said, turning back to his bed, "what will he do? How will he ever take care of his orchard?" Dad said nothing. I sat beside him for a few minutes more; then satisfied that he was all right, I left the house and walked into the orchard. The buds on the plums were beginning to swell. I knew their blossoms could not be far behind. I avoided the cherry trees once I heard the bees humming steadily as they gathered nectar and pollinated the trees. I knelt and balled up a handful of soil, then crumbled it and tossed its cool texture aside. I turned my face toward the mountains to the east. Fingers of white clouds caressed the tops of the hills. The wind freshened and lifted the bill of my cap. We will have rain, I thought.

Ginger called me from the back porch. "Rob, whatcha doing?"

"Checking on the orchard," I called back. "Mom's gone to the hospital. Hungry?"

"I fixed some cereal," she replied, her voice mixing with the whisper of wind in my ears.

"I'll be there in a minute." I waved to her, and she went back into the house. I looked at our house surrounded by trees and felt at that moment as if I never wanted to leave the safe haven it was to me. I rose from my knees and surveyed the orchard. *We'll be fine*, I thought, *just fine*.

After I returned to the house I helped Ginger gather the sheets from our beds and stuff them in our Bendix washing machine. "I hope we can get them dry before it rains," I said. By the time we were hanging them on the lines behind the house, Mom drove into the driveway.

"Any change?" I asked as she shut the car door behind her.

She shook her head. "They want Pauline to take him to a specialist next week. It's a good thing you're on Easter break so I can leave Dad with you."

I nodded my head. "How is Aunt Pauline?"

Mom reached up and clipped a clothes pin on one end of the sheet. "Not too well. I think she's overwhelmed." She smiled at me. "I know the feeling." We walked back into the house.

"How's Uncle Gus taking it?"

Mom's face darkened. "I don't know. He just sits there in his bed staring across his room." She sighed heavily. "The only thing he's said since they removed the dressings on his face was, 'I can't see.'"

She stood silently, leaning on the kitchen counter, gazing out the window at the sheets flapping gently in the breeze.

"Life's never simple, is it?"

"No, it isn't," she said, sighing again. "But you have to have faith. Without it . . ." her voice trailed off as she gazed unseeing into the orchard.

Ginger skipped into the kitchen. "When are we going to color our eggs?" she asked.

"Right now," said Mom, visibly brightening. "I'll put the eggs on to boil while you two get the dye ready." She slipped out of her coat and reached into the cabinet above the stove where she had hidden a box of Easter egg coloring. She handed it to me. "You know how to do this, don't you, son?"

"Sure," I said, going to the cupboard and bringing six

cups to the table. I placed a color tablet in the bottom of each cup and dissolved them in a teaspoon of vinegar while water was boiling on the stove. Half an hour later a dozen brightly colored eggs were drying on the windowsill.

The breeze had stiffened, and the sheets were flapping briskly on the line when the first drops of rain splattered against the window. Mom and I rushed outside and gathered the sheets off the clothesline. Like sails of a clipper ship, they billowed in the wind and carried us into the house. We spread them over the couch and chairs in the living room to let them finish drying. But then the rain stopped and the wind died, although clouds billowed above us.

"Help me turn your father," Mom said as she walked toward his room with Ginger following in her wake.

I have often thought since that momentous things happen without the clash of cymbals or the beating of drums. Usually they occur in the most innocuous and mundane moments, and we understand the impact only when we view it from the summit in the future.

We rotated Dad onto his side, and as Mom reached to straighten the tubing attached to his arm, I saw his eyelids flicker. An electric shock ran through me, and I shook my head to make sure I had not imagined it, but as I inspected his face, his eyelids flickered a second time.

"Mom," I said urgently. No cymbals or drums.

"What?" she asked wearily, continuing with her task.

But before I could answer, Dad's eyes blinked open, and he tried to lift his head.

"Dad!" Ginger screeched.

Slowly Dad shook his head from side to side as if trying to clear the cobwebs and blinked his eyes. Then he struggled to push himself up. My mother's mouth dropped open, and she enveloped him in her arms and helped him to sit. "Oh, John," she whispered with tears running down her cheeks. Outside the wind began gusting again, blowing a few raindrops against the window.

Dad raised his hand and rubbed his eyes. A puzzled look crossed his face as he looked at the plastic tube attached to the back of his hand. Slowly he focused on each of our faces and then smiled.

He struggled to clear his throat. He swallowed and rubbed his neck with his hand. "Is it Christmas morning yet?" he croaked in a voice barely above a whisper.

"Oh, yes, John. The best Christmas morning ever," said Mom as she gently hugged his frail frame and kissed him.

He blinked his eyes several times and wrinkled his forehead.

"Then where's the snow?" he asked, looking out the window. "It's not Christmas without snow."

In the orchard the breeze freshened and swirled through the cherry trees, combing their petals and sending a blizzard of blossoms against the bedroom window.

"Perfect, just perfect," smiled Dad.

"Mom?" said Ginger, pulling at Mom's skirt.

"What, Sweet Pea?"

"Can we open our presents?"

EPILOGUE

CASSANDRA JO, MY granddaughter, yawned and stretched as she sat on my lap. The snowflakes continued to fall outside our patio window onto the deck behind the house. "Did you have a nice nap, Cassy?" I asked.

She nodded her head. "It's still snowing."

"Yes it is. It's beautiful, isn't it? Your mom and dad ought to be here soon."

Again she nodded her head. "When will Great-Granpa get here?"

As if in answer to her question, the front door opened. "Anybody home? I understand a man can get a meal here," called out my dad.

"In the family room," I answered as Cassandra Jo jumped from my lap and ran into the front room to greet him.

Even at eighty-five years of age, my father walked briskly into the family room, carrying my granddaughter in his arms. My mother followed him, face beaming. She was brushing the snow from her hair.

"Can't even see it, Elizabeth," teased my father. "It's the same color as your hair."

"At least I have hair," she replied.

My father ran his hand over his head, now completely bald except for a few stray hairs at the nape of his neck, the ancient scar barely visible above his right ear. I pushed myself up from the recliner to hug the two of them.

"Looks like it will be a little while before we can prune the trees," I said, indicating the snow.

He flexed his hand. "Soon enough though."

Cassandra squirmed down from my father's arms. "I'll go tell Gramma Joan you're here," she said, running toward the kitchen.

"Rob," my mother said, putting her hand on my elbow, "we've become a terrible burden on you."

"Not at all," I said as I patted her hand.

"Still, it's nice to have you and Joan living next door all these years."

"Well," I replied, "after you and Dad bought Uncle Gus's place, I knew you couldn't handle it without my help." I chuckled. "Of course, after Joan and I married, moved in, and had our own brood, we had to remodel and enlarge the house."

"It solved a lot of problems, you know," Mom said. "It gave Pauline enough money to take care of Gus. And it gave us enough acreage to support both our families." Her voice trailed off, and I saw her gazing out the window at the falling snow. "It's too bad he lived only two years after the accident," she sighed. "And then Pauline followed so quickly."

"I think she wanted it that way," I said. "They needed to be together."

My father put his arm around my mother's shoulders, and together they gazed out through the French doors, across the patio, toward the orchard, only faintly illuminated by the yard light.

"I can understand that," my mother said quietly, looking up at Dad.

The snowflakes clung to the branches of the cherry trees as if they were in blossom. "Just look at that. Perfect," said my father. "Just perfect."